Follett 9/00

T3-BPD-450

MOONSHINE

Gary L. Blackwood

TECUMSEH MIDDLE SCHOOL
LIBRARY MEDIA CENTER

MARSHALL CAVENDISH • NEW YORK

Copyright © 1999 by Gary L. Blackwood
All rights reserved.
Marshall Cavendish Corporation
99 White Plains Road
Tarrytown, NY 10591

Library of Congress Cataloging-in-Publication Data:
Blackwood, Gary L.
Moonshine / Gary L. Blackwood.
     p. cm.
Summary: During the Depression, in the Ozarks of Missouri, thirteen-year-old
Thad has adventures selling moonshine and fishing with a rich visitor.
ISBN 0-7614-5056-4
1. Depressions—1929—Juvenile fiction.   [1. Depressions—1929—Fiction.
2. Ozark Mountains—Fiction. 3. Missouri—Fiction. 4. Fishing—Fiction.
5. Poverty—Fiction.] I. Title.
PZ7.B53338Mo 1999 [Fic]—dc21   99-10756   CIP

The text of this book is set in 12 point Stempel Garamond.
Book design by Constance Ftera
Printed in the United States of America
First edition

6 5 4 3 2 1

For Jean,
who hikes the hills and hollows with me

1

Thad had just finished digging up the Mason jar full of corn liquor when he heard the crackle of tires on gravel. He jerked his head up. The sheriff's red '28 Ford roadster was coming up over a rise in the road.

"God durn it!" Thad waved both hands frantically at the tourister, telling him to get out of there. The man started up his big Chrysler and roared away, flinging up gravel in his wake.

Thad hesitated a few seconds, making sure Sheriff Rickett wouldn't pull the tourister over. Then he snatched up the Mason jar and, holding it cradled in the crook of one arm like a football, scrambled down the hill, away from the road.

Normally he was as surefooted as a goat, but he wasn't used to wearing the bulky brogans. The lace of one of the shoes snagged on a wild grapevine and he went flying arse over tin cup and rolled for several yards before he fetched up against a hickory sapling.

The Mason jar burst, spraying him with corn liquor and shards of glass. "Oh, lordy," Thad groaned. Holding his ribs, he sat up painfully. His right forearm felt like he'd been bit by a stinging lizard. He lifted the arm gingerly and saw that there was a tear in the sleeve of his plaid shirt. The fabric around it was turning dark red.

Carefully Thad unbuttoned the sleeve and rolled it back. A neat triangle of glass was stuck in his arm, an inch or two to one side of the big vein. He fished his bandanna from the bottle pocket of his overalls. Then, gritting his teeth, he took hold of the glass shard and yanked it from his arm. Blood welled from the gash. He clamped the balledup bandanna over it.

Holding the injured arm tight against his chest, he searched among the rocks and the remains of last year's leaves for the zinc Mason jar lid. Dayman was going to be unhappy enough with him for losing a good jar and five dollars worth of corn whiskey. The least he could do was bring him back the lid.

Though the woods were beginning to turn dusky, he managed to locate the lid. He knocked loose the bits of glass that clung to the rubber seal, stuck the lid in his bottle pocket, and headed down the hollow for home.

After a time he gingerly lifted the bloodsoaked bandanna and checked on the cut. A little blood still seeped from it, but not enough so he had to worry.

Momma wasn't going to be happy to see the damage he'd done to one of his few decent shirts. Maybe he could soak the bloodstain out and mend the sleeve himself without her knowing. It wouldn't be the first time he'd kept something from her that would only have made her fret more if she knew.

Of course she'd only find something else to fret over. That was her way. Personally he couldn't see why she used up so much energy worrying about things. They'd always made out well enough. They always had food to eat, even if it was only squirrel and poke greens. And they had a roof over their heads, even if it did leak some when it rained particularly hard.

They didn't have much beyond the basics, it was true. But then how many folks in McDonald County did? In fact, he'd heard touristers say that times were hard not just in Missouri but all around the country. The Depression, they called it. You would scarcely have known it, though, from the way some of those touristers spread money around. They laid out more to stay at a local resort for a week or two, sometimes, than Thad and his momma saw in a good year.

They could have used the dollar Dayman would have given him as payment for bringing his goods to the customer—or, more accurately, bringing the customer to the goods.

Earlier that summer, when Dayman had first entrusted him with a jar of liquor, he'd been so foolish as to carry it in a poke right onto the dance pavilion at Shadow Lake and ask if anybody wanted to buy it. Frank Loveless had shooed him off and told him never to do that again. "You can't tell about these outlanders, boy," he had said when they were out of earshot. "They might turn you in to the revenuers. They might even *be* revenuers, for all you know."

Thad had slouched off, disappointed that his first attempt at salesmanship had turned out so badly. But before he was half a mile up the road, a fancy automobile pulled up next to him and the driver called out the window, "Is that moonshine any good?"

"Come again?" Thad said.

"The moonshine." The man pointed at Thad's poke. "Isn't that what you call it?"

"No sir. Moonshine is what we call fool talk, like when you tell a story that don't make no sense, or ain't strictly the truth." He lifted the poke. "This here we generally just call corn liquor. And I ain't never tasted it. My momma would kill me if'n I did. But there's folks that swear by it."

The man glanced around, as if to be certain they weren't being watched. "How much?"

"A Mason jar full."

The man laughed. "No, I mean how much are you charging."

"Oh." Thad hesitated. Five dollars sounded like an awful lot of money for a jar of anything except maybe gold. But that was what Dayman had said to ask for it. "Five dollars?" he said.

The tourister didn't blink an eye. He just pulled out his fat wallet, counted off five ones, and thrust them at Thad, who handed the poke in through the car window. "Oh, here," the man added, and pressed a fifty-cent piece into his hand. "For your trouble."

Thad had been so stunned he hadn't even thought to say "I'm obliged" until the man was long gone.

He still got what the touristers referred to as a "tip" from time to time. But more often he got an argument about the price. He'd learned never to let himself be talked down, though. After all, as Dayman said, where else were they going to get whiskey in a dry county?

In the end they always paid the asking price, though why they were so eager to get hold of something that tasted so much like kerosene was beyond Thad's understanding. He'd never actually sampled any kerosene, of course, but he had tried a sip of the corn liquor once, and only once, and had concluded that it was better suited for lamp fuel than for human consumption.

He'd also concluded that the best way of handling the

transactions was to conceal the Mason jar alongside a back road, then escort the customer to it. He'd gotten to ride in some very impressive vehicles that way. Some were so plush inside, they put him in mind of the expensive coffins he'd seen at the funeral parlor.

It seemed to Thad that Dayman would have done better just to handle the selling for himself, but he'd never said so to Dayman's face. If the man wanted to pay him to do it, who was he to argue?

He suspected that Dayman just didn't much care to associate with other folks. Most likely Thad would never have known the man existed if he hadn't stumbled across Dayman's still one day while roaming the woods. Since that first meeting he'd seen Dayman in Pineville only once, and that was early in the morning, when most townfolk were still abed.

Dayman managed somehow to keep himself supplied with shelled corn for making his sweet mash. When he required something else, such as tobacco or sugar or yeast, he asked Thad to fetch it for him.

Thad had never told his momma about Dayman or the liquor business, knowing she'd disapprove. He kept a little of the money Dayman paid him, for fishhooks and sweets and such as that, but turned most of it over to Momma to help with household expenses. Each time he concocted some bit of moonshine to explain how he'd come by the money. Touristers made the best cover story. They had a reputation for foolishly throwing their money around, and he took advantage of it.

To hear him tell it, touristers had readily rewarded him for performing such services as baiting hooks, gutting and scaling sunfish, finding arrowheads, fetching groceries, helping to push an automobile from a ditch, and giving directions to various local attractions such as Saltpeter Cave or the remains of Noah's Ark, which were reputed to be lodged in a gravel bar on Big Sugar Creek.

Like most good stories, these were not out and out lies. The truth was, he had done every one of those things over the course of the summer. He just hadn't accepted payment for any of them. His motives weren't entirely unselfish. He'd found that, by doing folks a good turn, he gained their trust, and they were more likely then to discuss with him matters of questionable legality, such as where to find a reliable source of corn liquor.

By the time Thad reached home, it was nearly dark. He turned down the alley behind their little house and approached it from the rear, meaning to put the shirt aside to soak before his momma saw it, or smelled it.

He'd left his bluetick hound, Dauncey, tied up by the house so the dog wouldn't follow him. Dauncey didn't like being left behind. Momma had rescued him when he was just a pup who would have died had she not brought him home and cared for him. Thad had claimed him, and ever since then Dauncey had been at his side almost continually, except for the hours that Thad grudgingly spent in school. But he couldn't very well take the dog along in a tourister's fancy automobile.

As soon as Dauncey caught his scent, the hound ran to the end of his chain, wriggling and wagging and whining. Thad knelt down and rumpled the dog's droopy ears affectionately. When Dauncey got a whiff of the alcohol-soaked shirt he backed off, shaking his head and sneezing.

Thad laughed softly. "I don't smell that bad, do I?" He unbuckled his overall straps and was about to shed the shirt when the crippled screen door at the rear of the house swung open and his momma stepped out. Shading her eyes from the light of the kerosene lamp in the kitchen, she peered into the dark. "I thought that'd be you."

"How'd you hear me?" Thad wanted to know.

"I didn't, but I heard Dauncey's tail thumping agin the wall. Where you been so late?"

"Late? It can't be more than half past nine."

"But you've been gone all day long. You're only thirteen, Thaddeus. It ain't right for you to be off all the time without telling me where."

"I wasn't no place in particular. Just around, same as always."

"What's that smell?"

"Kerosene," Thad said matter-of-factly. "I was fetching some for a feller and spilled it on my shirt."

"Put it to soak, then, and come on inside. We got company."

"Company? Who?"

"Pearly Rickett."

Thad stiffened. Pearly was Sheriff Rickett's brother. He was also the deputy sheriff. "What's he want?"

"Just a social call. He brought some coffee."

"I'll be in. I got to feed Dauncey first."

"I give him some scraps from the café already." His momma went back inside, leaving Thad standing there in the dark, speculating on what the real reason behind Pearly Rickett's visit might be.

2

He untied Dauncey, who gamboled about the yard, relishing his freedom. Thad pumped some fresh drinking water for the dog, then took down the galvanized washtub and filled it with water to soak the shirt. After he'd doused his hair and washed the chiggers off his legs, he rinsed out his bandanna and bound up the cut on his arm.

Momma and Pearly were sitting at the rickety kitchen table, drinking coffee from the thick, chipped mugs that Momma had brought home from Charles' Café, where she waited tables sometimes during tourist season, when business was brisk.

"Howdy, son." Pearly grinned, giving Thad an unpleasant view of uneven, tobacco-stained teeth. Whatever the reason his folks had named him Pearly, it was certainly not on account of his teeth. On the whole, though, the deputy looked more presentable than usual. His sparse hair was newly trimmed and slicked down with Brylcreem. A plaid bow tie was clipped crookedly to the collar of a shirt that was only marginally whiter than his teeth. Pinned to the shirt pocket, making it sag, was his deputy's badge. Below it several shirt buttons threatened to give way under the pressure of his paunch.

"How do," said Thad cautiously, wondering if Pearly's friendly demeanor was just an act. If his brother the sheriff had caught sight of Thad alongside the road, he might have guessed what he was up to, and sent Pearly here to try and trip him up.

"Brought some coffee. Like some?"

"I reckon not."

"Go on and have some, Thad," his momma urged. "It's good. A sight better than Postum, for certain."

"I don't care for any." Since their two wired-together chairs were in use—Pearly's was, in fact, creaking ominously under his weight—Thad pulled up the crude step stool his momma, who was a small woman, used to reach the highest of the board shelves that held their victuals and kitchen utensils.

"You been a-swimming?" Pearly asked, glancing at Thad's wet hair and the damp front of this overalls.

"No sir."

"Thought you might of been. Weather like this, the river's the best place to be. I mind when I was your age, I used to spend pretty near the whole day in the pond above the mill."

"Is that so?" Thad said.

Pearly bobbed his head at the bandanna bandage. "You hurt yourself?"

Thad shrugged. "Briar scratch is all."

There was a long silence. A moth that had found its way in through the torn screen now found the kerosene lamp and fluttered around the chimney, scorching its wings. Momma caught the moth in her cupped hands, took it to the screen door, and launched it into the dark.

"That door could use some mending," Pearly observed. "I could do it for you, if'n you like."

"Well, now—" Momma began, but Thad interrupted.

"No need to. I was set to do it myself."

Pearly nodded slowly. "Lucky it ain't a bad year for mosquitoes; too hot and dry, I guess."

Momma fanned herself with her apron. "It's hot all right, and so dry I give up on having a garden back in June."

There was another awkward silence. Pearly drained his coffee cup and got to his feet. "Well. I ought to do a turn around the town, make sure everything's battened down and shipshape." Pearly had served in the navy briefly during the Great War and, so no one should forget, he liked to make use of nautical terms at every opportunity.

Momma rose, too. "We're obliged for the coffee, Mr. Rickett." She held out the paper poke, which still contained a half pound or so.

"No, now, that's for you-uns to keep. I got plenty." He clapped on his slouch hat and said good night. Momma showed him out. When she returned, she wore a look of disapproval.

"You could of been a sight more sociable."

"I didn't care for his manner," Thad said, sullenly. "He kept on asking me questions."

"He was just trying to make conversation."

"And what about the coffee, and him offering to fix things around the house? He acts as though he's courting you or something."

"Would that be so awful? Plenty of women who've lost a husband go on and marry up again. I'm not an old woman, you know, not just yet."

Thad scowled. "I know that, but—"

"Besides, I believe having a man around would be a good thing for you. When there's just me, I can't keep a rein on you. I never know where you are, who you're with, what you're up to."

"I ain't doing nothing to be ashamed of."

"Ain't you? Pearly Rickett says he seen you the other day getting out of some tourister's automobile."

"The man offered me a ride, and I took it, that's all."

"And he paid you for the privilege, I guess."

"No."

"Pearly says he seen money change hands. I don't expect you were paying *him*."

"No! He wanted to know where was a good fishing hole, and I told him, and he give me a fifty-cent tip. I put it in there." He indicated the lard tin on the shelf that served as their bank.

"Well," his momma said, more subdued, "God knows we can use any extra money you bring in. I'd just like to know you're coming by it honestly."

"Like I said, I ain't doing nothing to be ashamed of."

She sighed. "I hope that's so. I worry that you might fall in with the wrong sort of people."

"Mostly the only company I keep is Dauncey, and he ain't likely to be a bad influence."

Momma laughed. "I reckon not."

"Besides, what about the company you keep? Pearly Rickett ain't my idea of the right sort of people."

"He may not be good looking, but he is respectable, and he is one of the few men in the county with a regular job."

"Then how come he can't afford a new set of teeth?"

Momma gave him a look of exasperation that barely concealed a smile. "It ain't nice to poke fun at folks."

"I'm just saying that you can do a whole lot better than the likes of Pearly Rickett."

"Well, I got no plans to marry the man. But I can still be sociable. And so can you."

In the morning Thad woke before Momma. He lit the small kerosene stove they used in hot weather, and set about making a pot of corn meal mush—not his favorite food, but it would do. Though there was no milk, there was a little oleomargarine left to top it with, and some sorghum molasses to drizzle on it.

As they sat down at the table, Momma said, "I'm to go in and work a couple hours at lunchtime. If 'n I get any tips, I'll buy us a few things."

"I ought to be able to bring home a red squirrel or a rabbit," Thad said. "Not much use trying to fish when it's this hot. They just hole up. Ples Morgan claims he can noodle a big catfish out from under a rock with just his hands, but any time I tried it all I got was a swole-up hand from a catfish spine." He went to the sink to rinse out his bowl, and gazed out the window at the ridge south of town, where he'd more than once seen a flock of wild turkeys. "I wish I had me a shotgun, or even a twenty-two. I'd bring home all the game we could eat. " He turned to Momma." Why didn't my daddy have a gun he could have left me?"

"Your daddy didn't like guns. He wouldn't have one in the house."

"Why not? He must of had to shoot a gun in the War, didn't he?"

Momma stared down at her bowl, tracing patterns in the melted oleo with her spoon. "I reckon so. He never said. He didn't like to talk much about the War."

"And you don't like to talk about him much, do you?"

"There ain't much to talk about. He didn't stay around long."

"You reckon he's still alive somewhere?"

She gave him a sharp glance. "You keep on asking me that. If 'n he is, he don't want us to know where, or else he'd of got in touch. Now let's drop it, can we?"

"Yeah, sure." Thad pulled on his brogans and tied them. "See you at dinner, I guess."

"You want to give me some idea where you might be?"

"I don't know myself. No place in particular."

"Well, don't you go too deep in the woods. Folks say a panther's been spotted down toward Southwest City."

"That sounds like moonshine to me. If 'n there was a panther, he'd be tearing up folks' livestock, wouldn't he?"

"Maybe. But Pearly Rickett also says that somebody killed a possum with rabies the other day."

"Stop fretting, Momma. I'll be fine."

"I just want to you be careful," she said. "You're the only boy I got."

Dauncey was waiting outside and ran eagerly ahead of him down Dog Hollow hill. Though it wasn't yet nine o'clock, some of the boys his age were playing baseball in the field across from the school, getting their practicing in before the heat got too bad.

"Thad!" Clem Cordell called to him as he neared the field. "Come on and pitch a few!"

Thad waved a hand at him. "You don't need me."

"We do so. We play the Cassville team this evening, and I hear the pitcher has an arm on him. These fellers need some practice swinging at some real fastballs."

"Hey!" protested Billy Ed Bradley, from the pitcher's mound. "What do you call what I been throwing?"

"Well, no offense Billy Ed, but my little sister can throw that hard. Thad's fastball will scorch your eyebrows—or at least it would, if'n he didn't always put it in the strike zone."

Thad stolled across the road to the ball field. Dauncey lay down in the grass to wait for him. As much as Dauncey doted on Thad, he never wanted to have anything to do with other people or other dogs. "Shoot," Thad said, "I can't pitch. Now Bib Tarkey, he could pitch."

"Who's Bib Tarkey?" Billy Ed wanted to know.

"Ain't you heard of Bib Tarkey? He used to be the blacksmith here. He once threw a ball so hard it knocked the web right out of the catcher's glove, shot all the way across the road there, and bored a hole in the hillside so deep you can't touch the end of it with a fishing pole. Some claim it's so deep that if'n you put your ear up to it, you can hear folks talking Chinese."

Billy Ed snorted. "I don't believe that. I don't believe none of it."

Thad shrugged. "The hole's still there. I can show it to you." He walked to the edge of the road and beckoned to Billy Ed. "See straight across there?"

Billy Ed peered at the hillside. "Why, that's nothing but an old woodchuck hole."

"It is now, sure. If you was a woodchuck, and seen a ready-made hole, wouldn't you move in? It's easier than digging a new one."

"Come on, Thad," Clem Cordell pleaded. "Quit your moonshining and do some pitching."

Thad took the worn baseball from him and walked out to the dusty mound. Billy Ed picked up the battered wooden bat and stepped up to the buried cinder block that was home plate. "All right, McCune, let's see what you got."

Clem winked at Thad. "No beanballs now, you hear?"

Billy Ed took a step back, looking worried. "I thought you said he always puts them in the strike zone."

"Well, nobody's perfect." Clem crouched down behind the plate. "Let her rip, Thad."

Thad saw no call to warm up. He didn't bother to wind up, either. That had always seemed to him like showing off. He just drew back and flung the ball, the way he'd chuck a stone at a red squirrel. It zipped across the center of the cinder block, belt high, and smacked into Clem's ancient catcher's mitt with a sound like a twenty-two shot.

"Yow!" Clem hollered, and shook the hand with the mitt on it as he tossed the ball back to the mound. "Wait a second, would you?" He took out his bandanna and stuffed it in the mitt. "Okay."

Thad burned another one across. Billy Ed looked like he couldn't decide whether to swing or to get out of the way. On the third pitch, Billy Ed gave a halfhearted swing, but didn't make contact. He threw the bat down in disgust and stomped off.

"I told you he was fast, didn't I?" Clem called. "Next victim!"

Gene Butterworth stepped up. Though he clenched his teeth and chased every pitch, the most he got was a foul tip. "God durn," he said, shaking his head. "I wish you was pitching for us."

"I'll say," put in Archie Obler. "We'd have the championship sewed up. What about it, Thad?"

"Might as well not waste your breath, boys," Clem said glumly. "I've tried fifty times to talk him into it. And Coach Lane has done everything but threaten his life to get him to play for the school team."

"What's the matter with you, McCune?" demanded Billy Ed. "Ain't you got no loyalty?"

Thad grinned good-naturedly. "I reckon not." He tossed the ball high in the air and caught it. "I don't know, fellers, it just all seems too much like work to me."

Billy Ed made a sour face. "I'm glad I ain't as lazy as you."

"Well, I'm glad I ain't as foul tempered as you." Thad flipped the ball underhand to Clem. "That's enough, I reckon. I got to save my arm for the squirrels."

He started off the field, but Clem caught up with him. "You know, you could bring down a lot more game if'n you had yourself a gun."

"I expect so. But guns cost money."

"Well, I'll tell you; I got an old twenty-two I could let you have for . . . say, six dollars. It don't look good, but it does shoot straight."

"Might as well be six hundred."

"Now let me finish. I was about to say I'd knock it down to four if'n you was to do something for me in return."

"Let me guess. You want me to pitch for the Pineville Panthers."

Clem grinned. "I always said you was quick. So, what do you say?"

"I'll think about it. Four dollars is hard to come by."

"I'd give it to you for nothing, being as I don't ever use it, but my daddy would skin me. You know how he is."

"Hey, Clem!" Gene Butterworth called. "Haul your overalls back over here!"

"Got to go." Clem clapped Thad on the shoulder. "Don't think about it too long, okay? The playoffs are in a couple of weeks."

The pavement around the square felt hot already, even through the soles of his brogans. Though he didn't like wearing the shoes, which were too tight, a person needed something on his feet since they'd put down the concrete streets and sidewalks. He didn't care much for the concrete, either, but it did keep the streets from turning into mud baths when it rained—presuming it ever did decide to rain again.

The pavement had been a project of Mr. Roosevelt's Works Progress Administration, and had provided temporary work for some of the men in the county last fall and winter. There were precious few other opportunities for a person to put some cash money in his pockets.

Making corn liquor was a possibility, of course, but it

wasn't a trade that was suited to just anyone. It required a willingness to sit all alone in the woods somewhere for weeks on end, tending a cantankerous still that, if you didn't treat it just right, was liable to blow itself up, and you along with it.

Then, too, there was the fact that it was highly illegal. It wasn't the alcohol itself that was outlawed, as it had been during Prohibition. It was the making of it without a proper license, and without paying the required taxes, that the government didn't like.

Neither Sheriff Rickett nor his brother Pearly was likely to go to all the trouble of actually tramping through the woods looking for the location of a still. What they were likely to do was confiscate any corn liquor they came across, so it was wise to steer clear of them.

There were maybe half a dozen folks in the county who made a reasonable living through mostly legal means. J.E. Houseman, who owned the hardware and lumber-yard, was one. There wasn't all that much money to be made from selling boards and nails, considering that so few folks could afford to build anything more ambitious than a new two-hole backhouse.

Thad suspected that a good deal of Mr. Houseman's wealth came from his buying up land that was being auctioned off for back taxes, then selling it for ten times what he'd paid for it to touristers who had spent a few weeks at Shadow Lake or Ginger Blue and imagined they'd like to retire in the Ozarks.

Thad stopped before one of the plate glass windows that J.E. Houseman had installed last year, under the metal sign he'd had made in Springfield, which read

"Houseman Lumber & Hardware. For All Your Building Needs See The House Man." As if there was anybody else in Pineville they *could* see.

He stood at the edge of one of the big windows, so as not to be conspicuous, and shaded his eyes to peer through the glass. Willa Houseman was inside, straightening up a rack of vegetable seeds. There was no sign of her mother or father. She looked so serious and intent on her task that Thad grinned. For as long as Thad had known her—and that was most of their lives—she'd gone at everything, from an arithmetic test to a game of mumblety-peg, that same way, as if her life depended on her doing it just so.

"You wait here, Dauncey," Thad said. The dog flopped down agreeably next to the entrance. Thad stepped inside the store carefully, so the bell above the door wouldn't make a racket. It clanked softly, and he reached one long arm up and muffled it with his hand.

Willa spun around. "Thad!"

Thad put a finger to his lips and glanced around. "Where's your folks?"

"Father's out looking at property. Mother's in the back, giving the yardmen what for. She's liable to be a while. Come on in."

Thad relaxed and moved over next to her. "Surely you don't sell many of them seeds this late in the summer."

"Hardly any. I'm just sorting them out for something to do. Things are awful slow. What are you up to?"

"Not much. Thought I might go on up to our old place. I ain't been there in a while."

"To Sinking Spring?" She bit her lip and wrinkled her

23

forehead in distress. "Oooh, I wish I could go with you."

"There's nothing keeping you from it. You said things was slow."

"My folks would have a fit and fall in it."

"You don't have to tell them, do you?"

"I ain't going to lie."

"Not telling ain't the same as lying. They sure don't like me much anymore do they? Time was you and me spent practically all day every day together, and they never said ary word agin it."

Willa smiled wistfully. "We was younger then. My folks say it's time I started behaving more like a lady."

"How does a lady behave, exactly?"

Willa laughed. "I ain't just sure. But I don't guess that swinging from a grapevine or catching crawdads or dressing in overalls is supposed to be part of it."

Thad shook his head. "It can't be much fun, then. How do they figure I ought to behave?"

"They never come right out and said." She put a hand on his arm. "It ain't that they don't like you. They just think you're a little too . . . well, you know. Wild."

"Wild? Makes me sound like some kind of animal—a wolf or a black bear or the like."

"Well, you spend as much time in the woods as any bear. Besides, it ain't just that. They think I'm getting to an age where I shouldn't be alone with boys."

"Any boys, or just particular ones? I bet they'd fret a lot less about it if'n I was a lawyer's son, or a doctor's, and not just some woods colt."

She elbowed him lightly in the ribs. "Don't be calling yourself that. Your momma and daddy was married."

"Even so, I might as well have no daddy. I don't know where he is. I hardly know who he is." Thad had never even met any of his daddy's family. He wasn't sure where they could be found. He didn't know his momma's family much better. He couldn't recall ever hearing the names of but two or three. His momma rarely spoke of them. It was as if he had no kin except for her.

"Well," Willa said, "I know well enough who my father is, and that don't make him any nicer. At least when you don't know, you can imagine he's somebody special."

Thad examined a packet of squash seeds without really looking at it and softly said, "I do that sometimes. Sometimes I tell myself that he didn't just up and run off at all, that he had some purpose in mind, like maybe he's a prospector up in the Klondike, and when he strikes it rich, he'll . . " Thad paused and laughed at himself. "But all the time I know it's just so much moonshine."

"Maybe not, though," Willa said eagerly. "He could be anything. He could be a movie star. Maybe he's Errol Flynn. They say he's had dozens of affairs."

"I don't reckon he's ever passed through Pineville, though. And so far as I know my momma has never been to Hollywood. Besides, my daddy's name was John; I know that much."

"That don't mean nothing. Actors change their names all the time. Maybe he just changed his last name. Maybe he's John Wayne. No, John Wayne's real name was Marion, as I recall. Oh, I didn't tell you, did I? I seen him last night, at the theater in Anderson."

"He was in Anderson?"

"Not in person, silly. In a motion picture. He's so

handsome. Not as good looking as Errol Flynn, of course, or Robert Taylor. More sort of . . . rugged looking."

Thad nodded silently. He never knew what to say when she began going on about moving pictures, as she had been doing increasingly the past year or so. He'd only ever seen one that he could recall, and he'd been no more than five or six at the time.

"Minnie Brewer and her folks took me. Oh, I wish you could of come, too. It was . . . it was . . ." She searched for a word to describe it, then threw up her arms. "I don't know how to say what it was. When I see a good picture, I feel as if I'm being swept away into another world, one that's funnier and more exciting and more romantic than this one, and I wish I could just stay." She looked around at the mundane interior of the store, then up at Thad. "Do you know what I mean?"

Though he didn't exactly, he thought it wouldn't do to say so. "I reckon. It's sort of like a windy."

"A what?"

"You know, a tall tale. Most of the things that happen in them are bigger than life."

Willa frowned. "Well, that's so. But everyone knows when they're listening to a tall tale that it ain't supposed to be true. With motion pictures it's different. For the hour or two that you're watching one, it's more than just a story. It's real."

"That don't mean it's true," Thad started to say. Then he heard the back door of the store open and close. Quickly he stepped away from Willa's side and pretended to be looking over the new selection of plumbing fixtures. At least he guessed that's what they were. His familiarity with indoor plumbing was about as extensive as his knowledge of moving pictures. Willa abruptly turned her attention back to the seed rack.

Mrs. Houseman emerged from the back room and stared at Thad, narrow-eyed. "Did you want something, Thaddeus?" she asked, not cordially at all.

To be treated like a person would be nice, he thought, but he said, "Yes'm. I was wanting to get me a whetstone."

"Well, we don't keep them among the plumbing supplies. They are over here." She pointed to a display behind the counter. "The cheapest one we have is ten cents."

"Well, I believe I'll take this here fifteen cent one," Thad said, just to show her, though it was all the money he had. She didn't even wrap it.

As he went out the door, he glanced in Willa's direction. She smiled warily and waved good bye, but he noticed that she kept her hand close to her chest, as though hiding the gesture from her mother's view.

4

As soon as he got past the last cluster of houses that lay south of the square, Thad stopped and took off the brogans and tossed them inside an old rusty Model T Ford with no wheels, which sat up on cinder blocks. He'd been wearing the shoes a lot lately. He didn't like to go around to the resorts, taking orders for Dayman's corn liquor, without a shirt or shoes. It made the touristers want to take pictures of him, as if he was some local curiosity. As a result his feet weren't as tough as they ordinarily would be this late in the summer.

The coarse gravel alongside Big Sugar Creek made him walk a bit gingerly. He had to watch out for broken bottles, too. Why touristers came here to enjoy the creek and then left it littered with trash was beyond his understanding.

The creek was low from the lack of rain. He didn't even have to roll up the legs of his overalls to cross it. Dauncey waded into deeper water to cool off, and emerged shaking himself and spraying water all around.

In the woods the earth underfoot was dry as bleached bone. Thad hoped that Dayman and whoever else was running a still hereabouts were keeping a close eye on their wood fires. If one of them got careless, the flames would spread through these woods the way a bit of good gossip spread through the town.

It was an hour's hike to Sinking Spring, at a quick pace. It lay in an old, logged-over area far to the east of town. There were no roads near it except for a few overgrown logging traces, so hardly anyone ever passed that way, except for maybe a coon hunter now and again.

All around Sinking Spring the trees had been cut down for railroad ties years before. In their place brush had grown up head high and so dense that most folks were inclined to detour around it. That explained why almost no one aside from Thad and Willa knew that the spring even existed.

They had come upon it several years before, purely by accident. They had been hunting morel mushrooms, mostly without success. For some reason Willa had gotten it into her head that beyond the wall of brush was a clearing, and that the hypothetical clearing would prove to be thick with morels. Once a notion took hold of Willa there was no getting rid of it, so Thad had burrowed along behind her through the brush. Though his big frame had suffered innumerable scratches, Willa's slight body had emerged practically unscathed.

What lay beyond the brush was not a clearing but a sinkhole, a depression in the ground some forty to fifty feet across, where underground water had eaten away a cavity in the soluble limestone until finally the earth above the hole had collapsed.

On the uphill side of the depression, a trickle of water flowed from beneath a layer of limestone and into a small, clear pool before moving on and disappearing under a jumble of mossy rocks.

Willa had stood on the edge of the sinkhole, staring, with one hand held over her mouth. Thad had taken her by the arms, fearful that she might lose her footing and tumble headfirst down the steep side of the sinkhole. Finally she had said, almost in a whisper, "It's an enchanted place!"

As was often the case, Thad wasn't entirely sure of her meaning, but he knew better than to contradict her. They had put aside any thoughts of gathering morels and had spent the afternoon lounging by the spring, soaking their feet, eating the butter bread they'd brought along, washing it down with spring water, talking a little now and again, but mostly feeling no need to.

As the sun worked its way down the sky, Thad had begun to understand what Willa meant about this being an enchanted place. Though it was long past time for them to return home, he felt the hidden hollow pulling at him, reluctant to let him go. When they headed back at last, they had sworn that, from that day forward, this would be their secret, special place. They would never reveal its location or even its existence to anyone, no matter who, upon pain of death.

A few days later, Thad had come back with a borrowed pair of pruning shears and, beginning a yard or so from the outer edge of the brush, had cleared a path so they could make their way in to the sinkhole sanctum without doing damage to themselves and their clothes.

That was before Willa's folks came to regard him as unsuitable company for their daughter, and he and Willa had come to Sinking Spring together at least once a week. Each time they passed through the barrier of brush and emerged on the edge of the sinkhole, it was like entering a small, safe, self-contained world, a world that had no need of rules, or money, or schools, or jobs. Thad often felt that he could stay there in that little world indefinitely and be perfectly content, living on the cold, clear water and whatever small game came to drink at the spring.

But for Willa, Sinking Spring seemed to be something else—not a spot to stay in so much as a spot to dream in, someplace where she could weave plans for the future, knowing that, unlike her folks, Thad would listen and not scoff.

Sometimes it was hard for Thad to listen, though, because in all her plans there was no mention of Pineville and no mention of him. She talked instead of places and people she had seen on the moving picture screen, or read about in *Photoplay*. She spoke of these places just as if she'd been there, and of these people as if she knew them and they knew her and were out there waiting for her to reach an age when she could break away and join them.

Of course, half the boys and girls he knew talked about leaving, about finding something better. Clem planned to play for the Chicago White Sox; Virg Marney's heart was set on being a locomotive engineer; Billy Ed meant to enlist in the army as soon as he looked old enough to get away with it.

It made Thad uncomfortable when his friends talked that way; he felt as if he should have plans of his own. But he couldn't seem to think that far ahead, and didn't really care to.

As time went on and he and Willa were discouraged from seeing each other, Thad had gotten out of the habit of coming to the spring. Lately he'd found himself missing it, as much as he missed Willa. Though he didn't care to make trouble for her, he wished she could have seen her way clear to come.

As he strode along the ridge, Thad kept an eye out for good throwing stones. He liked them to be as round as possible, and to fit easily in his palm. His favorites were the lumps of sandstone that contained rusty patches of iron ore. They had a nice heft to them. But chert would do if the edges weren't too sharp.

When he was younger, he had experimented with weapons of various kinds—a slingshot made from a length of tubing bent into the shape of a Y, a bow made from a stick of Osage orange—but had concluded that the most dependable weapon—aside from a gun, which he couldn't hope to afford—was his own arm, and the best ammunition was rocks.

Certainly there was no danger of the supply ever running out. They were the only crop that truly flourished here. If only there were a market for rocks, everyone in the Ozarks would be a millionaire several times over. Thad had once heard a story about a real estate man who sold eighty acres of rock-infested land to a city fellow by convincing him that the rocks were a valuable commodity. "See there," the real estate man said, pointing to a farmer who was clearing rocks from a neighboring field, "there's a dad-blamed rock thief making off with some right now!"

Dauncey flushed out a rabbit and barked at several red squirrels, but each time Thad said, "No, come on, now." In this heat, meat went bad so fast he didn't want to bring down an animal until he was ready to eat it.

It was so long since he'd been to Sinking Spring, he had a little trouble locating the path he'd cleared. It was grown over some, but that was good. It showed that no one else had found their way in to the spring.

He pushed through the brush with Dauncey at his heels and climbed down the rock wall of the sinkhole. The drought had shrunk up the pool of water, but the spring hadn't dried up, as some had. While Dauncey lapped noisily at the water, Thad slipped off his overalls, took a sliver of lye soap from the bib pocket, and scrubbed his legs thoroughly. The chiggers weren't bad in a dry summer like this one, but even a few of the tiny red bugs could provide plenty of misery if you gave them a chance to dig in.

The springwater was so cold it raised gooseflesh. Dauncey took off exploring. Thad lay back on a warm, lichen-covered slab of limestone and let the sun dry him off. The heat made him drowsy and lethargic. He closed his eyes.

He had no idea how long he lay there in a sort of stupor before he heard the sound of something plowing through the brush on the hillside above him. Whatever was coming, it was something large. He knew it wasn't Dauncey; the hound moved almost soundlessly through the woods.

Thad recalled what his momma had said about the cougar being sighted and, despite the heat, a chilly prickle went up his spine. Suppose there really was a big cat prowling through the woods?

The crunching sounds grew louder. He could see the tops of the brush swaying. Thad snatched up his overalls and dug into the side pocket for one of the throwing stones he'd gathered. Crouching, clutching the rock in his right hand, he waited.

"Thad?" a voice called.

It was Willa. And here he was, wearing nothing but his underpants. "God durn it!" Thad muttered. He flung the rock aside and jammed one leg into his overalls. Then he hopped about frantically, trying to force his other leg into the remaining britch leg, which was turned half inside out.

He managed to wrestle the britches on and get one strap buckled before Willa appeared on the rim of the sinkhole. Her hair was disheveled and full of twigs and leaves. The knees of her riding britches were smeared with dirt, and one sleeve of her blouse was torn. "I couldn't find the path," she said, forlornly.

Scowling with embarrassment, Thad fumbled with the other strap of the overalls. "What are you doing here?"

She picked her way carefully down the side of the sinkhole, the heels of her riding boots clicking on the stones. "You could at least act glad to see me."

"I'm glad all right. I just didn't expect you. I thought you was a panther."

She laughed, and growled at him like a big cat.

"What did you tell your folks?" he said.

"I told them I was taking Tony out for a ride, which I am." Tony was her small appaloosa gelding, which she had named, she said, after Tom Mix's horse—whoever Tom Mix was. Willa sat next to him on the big rock and wiped at her forehead with a delicate white handkerchief. "Don't worry, I tied him down the hill a ways, like always, so I wouldn't leave a trail." She glanced around. "It don't look like anyone else has been in here."

"Not as far as I could tell."

She turned to look at him. "I ain't never told a single soul about the place, Thad. Have you?"

"Of course I ain't. I give my word that I wouldn't, didn't I?"

"Yes, but I thought you might of forgot."

"Not me."

She sighed and leaned back on the rock. "I'd almost

forgot how peaceful it was here. I believe this is the only place I'll truly miss."

"Miss? You planning to go someplace?"

She smiled at the worried tone in his voice. "Not right away, silly. When I go out on my own, I mean." She sat up. "Oh, I nearly forgot why I came out here."

"Besides to scare the wits out of me, you mean?"

"I have some big news to tell you. A little while after you left, Mrs. Mitchell came in the store to buy some wallpaper, and we got to talking, and guess what she told me."

"If I had to guess, I'd say something to do with moving pictures." Mrs. Mitchell, their English teacher, was almost as crazy about moving pictures and actors as Willa was.

"No, but it's close." She clapped both hands on his forearm as if fearing that what she was about to reveal might blow him away. "She's going to put on a school play! Ain't that marvelous?"

Thad scratched his head with his free hand. "Well, that ain't the word I would have used, but sure. I reckon she'll give you a big part."

Willa's eyes fairly gleamed. "Do you think so?"

"If'n she has any sense, she will. It ain't going to be that Shakespeare, is it?"

Willa laughed. "I don't expect Pineville is ready for Shakespeare. I can just picture myself as Juliet, though, can't you?" She struck a tragic pose.

"Well, I've got to say it's hard, with your hair that way."

"What way?" She ran her fingers through her tousled, twig-laden hair. "Ow!" She fished a comb from the pocket of her britches and began tugging at the tangles.

"Do you realize," she said, her eyes wide with excitement, "that this could be just the first step toward an illustrious career on stage and silver screen?" She flung her arms apart dramatically and the comb flew from her hand. Thad bent to retrieve it, but she said, "No!" and stuck out a foot and planted it on the comb. "Folks say you can make a wish on a dropped comb." She closed her eyes and smiled to herself as she framed a wish in her mind. When she opened her eyes, they were bright and mischievous. "Guess what I wished."

"I can't. It won't come true if'n I do."

"Then don't. Because I surely want it to come true."

"You'd best have wished that your folks don't find out where you run off to."

"They won't." She pulled the comb through her unruly hair again, wincing. "I guess you think I'm silly, making wishes that way."

He shrugged. "There's nothing wrong with making wishes, as long as you don't expect them to necessarily come true."

"Don't you ever make wishes, like on the first star in the evening, or a wishbone, or such as that?"

Thad shook his head. "Nope. Not generally."

"Why not?"

"I can't think of too much I want that I don't already have."

"Really?" Willa looked at him curiously. "You mean you're satisfied with things the way they are? Your life? This town?"

"Pretty much."

She sat staring at the comb a minute, pulling the

strands of her hair from it. "I find that very sad."

"Sad? Why?"

"You're smart, Thad, and you're good looking and nice. You could go far in the world. Instead you don't want nothing but to stay right where you are."

"It seems a whole lot sadder to me to always be wanting what you ain't got."

She turned to him slowly, with a hurt sort of look, as though he'd insulted her. Then she stood abruptly and brushed off the seat of her riding britches. "Well, it's time I got on home."

"Already? You ain't been here but ten minutes. Time was we used to spend the whole afternoon here."

"I know. I wish I still could."

"But that ain't what you wished on the comb, is it?"

She dropped her gaze. "No," she said. "I really do have to go, before my folks send out a search party." She started off, then stopped and half turned back. "If'n you want, you could ride back with me, on Tony. You could sit up behind, like you used to."

"Thanks, but I believe I'll stay."

"Suit yourself." She scrambled up the side of the sink-hole. At the top she stood for a moment, looking back and forth. Then she called plaintively over her shoulder, "Thad? Where's the path?"

"To your left," he said. "About three paces." She found it and, without another word, disappeared.

6

After Willa left, Thad felt unaccountably restless. More predictably, he also felt hungry. When Dauncey returned from exploring, they went in search of game.

It didn't take long for Dauncey to spook a red squirrel and send it scrambling up the trunk of an old oak. When it stuck its head around the tree to scold them, Thad was ready. He let fly with one of his throwing stones. It sent chips of bark flying about six inches above the squirrel's head, and sent the squirrel scurrying into the high branches, out of range. "God durn it!" Thad grumbled. He was used to missing his aim now and again, but not usually by that much.

He rubbed his elbow, which felt a little sore. He must have strained it, fooling around with that baseball. Well, he didn't feel much like going to the bother of skinning the critter and building a fire anyway, not in this heat. Maybe he could bring down an animal on the way home, and Momma could fix it for supper.

"Come on, Dauncey," he said. The hound gave him a quizzical look, as though wondering why they were letting a stupid squirrel get the best of them, and then loped after him.

Each time he visited Dayman's still, he took a slightly different route, to keep from wearing down a trial. But he'd never approached it from this direction before, and it took him some time to zero in on it. There was never any smoke to give away the still's location, for Dayman burned only seasoned hickory with the bark peeled off.

Dayman's hollow was an unusually deep and narrow one, of the sort that prompted folks to say that a dog couldn't wag its tail sideways there, only up and down. As such, it made a good hiding place for his still. It was unlikely that anyone would go to the trouble of exploring such a hollow unless he had a reason.

A small stream, all but dry in a summer like this, had carved its way through the limestone, leaving rock ramparts twenty feet high on either bank, and a streambed of stone nearly as broad and smooth as the new cement walks on the Pineville square. Dayman had erected his still on one of these level slabs, at a spot where a small but reliable spring trickled from between the layers of limestone.

The still was an ungainly-looking contraption that resembled the devices drawn by newspaper cartoonist Rube Goldberg. But unlike Mr. Goldberg's fanciful inventions, this one had a practical purpose, and had proven its utility through years of use.

Since Dayman wasn't the sort to go around explaining things, even when asked, Thad had had to work out for himself, with the help of the science he'd studied in school, how the still functioned.

The heart of the setup was a big copper tank called the cooker; it was perched on rocks, high enough to build a fire under it. In the cooker Dayman brought to a boil what he called the mash, which was nothing more than sprouted corn, ground up and mixed with warm water, then left to ferment for a couple of days. The alcohol from the mash turned into steam, which rose through a pipe in the top of the cooker, then into the thump keg, a barrel partly full of water. When the water in the keg reached the boiling point, it made a thumping sound.

After the alcohol vapor left the thump keg, it passed through the worm, a coil of copper pipe lying in a trough full of cold water from the spring. The alcohol condensed inside the worm and dripped out the end into a gallon glass jug.

Distilling corn liquor seemed to Thad the ideal way to make a living. It did entail a little physical labor—chopping up hickory chips, grinding the mash, filtering the finished liquor through charcoal—but the biggest share of the job, as far as he could see, was sitting by, watching the still do its work and making sure the mash didn't boil up in the cooker and clog the exit pipe, in which case the pressure would build up and burst the copper tank.

He'd heard that some whiskey makers strained the mash through a cloth and just boiled the liquid, to prevent the cooker clogging up. But Dayman was of the opinion that it made for a better product if you cooked it mash and all.

Another thing that appealed to Thad was the seasonal nature of the work. Dayman never operated his still any later than October or any earlier than May. It was too hard to keep the corn warm enough to sprout or to ferment. Thad gathered that, in the cold months, Dayman, with the still, hid away in a ramshackle shanty up on Razorback Ridge.

To Thad's mind the best features of the trade were the fact that it let a fellow spend all his time in the woods, and that he had only himself to answer to. He suspected that the solitude was what had attracted Dayman to it, too.

When Thad finally located the still, Dayman was hacking at a hickory limb with his ax. For a one-armed man he managed pretty well. The chips were flying like feathers in a henhouse when a fox is paying a visit. As always, he let Dauncey run on ahead, so as not to startle Dayman, who was deaf in one ear—from the same artillery shell that had taken off his arm, Thad guessed. It was one of the many things that Dayman had never felt motivated to explain.

Dayman had been in France during the Great War, Thad knew that much. He must have been awfully young at the time, for he couldn't be more than forty now. Most likely he had done as Billy Ed planned to do, and lied about his age.

It was hard to assign a definite age to Dayman. He walked stooped over like an old man, yet he was lithe and quick about his work. Unlike most men in the county, he let his hair and beard grow, and that masked his features some. So did the wide-brimmed hat he wore pulled down low on his forehead. There wasn't much gray in his beard, but above it, his face was etched with deep lines.

For some reason, Dayman was one of the few people that Dauncey took to. The hound trotted up to Dayman, panting and wagging his tail— and, contrary to what folks said, there was room for him to move it side to side. Dayman set the ax aside and knelt down to pat the dog's head. "Hey, boy," he said. "Hey."

Now that Thad's arrival had been announced, he came on up the hollow. "Howdy, Dayman!" he called. Dayman raised his sole hand in a greeting so brief that a person might not have noticed, then set about tossing chips into the fire under the cooker.

"How about I do some of that chopping for you?" Thad said, and took up the ax.

"If'n you want."

"Well, I figure it's the least I can do," Thad said as he attacked the hickory limb, "seeing as how I busted your Mason jar and lost five dollars worth of your product." Dayman didn't reply. Thad turned to him. Dayman was pounding the plug out of his corncob pipe and filling it with fresh tobacco from a pouch. "You hear what I said?"

"I heard. I don't reckon you did it a-purpose."

"Of course I didn't. I was trying to avoid Charley Rickett, and I fell down."

"That'll happen." Dayman lit his pipe with a sliver of hickory and puffed at it.

"I did bring back the lid." Thad dug it from his back pocket and handed it to Dayman, then went back to chopping up the hickory and scraping the chips into a pile. By the time he was done, he was drenched with sweat. "Anything else you want me to do?"

"I reckon not. Unless you care to sell another jar."

"You sure you trust me?"

Dayman seldom looked him in the eye. Mostly he behaved as though he were in some world all his own, one that Thad couldn't quite reach. When he spoke it was more as if he were talking to himself, or to Dauncey, or to the fire, and Thad just happened to overhear.

But this time Dayman raised his eyes and met Thad's. The man's eyes, Thad saw, were blue—not bright blue like

Thad's but a washed-out color like the sky on a cold day in December. "If'n I didn't trust you," he said, "you wouldn't be here right now."

Thad dropped his gaze. "I'll sell it for you without no charge until I've paid back the five dollars."

"Four," said Dayman, talking to himself again. "A dollar of that was yours."

"All right, then, four." Thad hiked up the straps of his overalls. "You got some ready to go now?"

"In the tent."

On a narrow strip of sand and gravel deposited by the stream, Dayman had pitched a canvas pup tent that looked as if it dated back to the Great War. Thad lifted one tent flap. Inside were several layers of old, frayed quilts folded up to make a bed. Next to them was a beat-up copy of *Wild Horse Mesa* by Zane Grey. That was all, except for two jars full of clear corn liquor.

"You might take both them jars," Dayman said to the bluetick hound, "and leave one in the sycamore stump for Ben Starnes."

"I'll do that." Thad tucked one Mason jar carefully under each arm. "You need anything from town?" He said it loudly enough, and he was on Dayman's good side, but the man didn't respond. "I take that to mean no. Come on, Dauncey. See you in a day or two." Dayman still made no reply, only puffed at his pipe and threw a handful of chips on the fire.

The sycamore stump was on a piece of bottomland not far from town. Thad lowered the Mason jar into the hollow stump and sprinkled bits of punky wood over top of it, then set a rock on the stump as a signal to Ben Starnes to look inside.

As he headed home, he debated over what to do with the second jar. From what Momma had said, it sounded as if the Rickett brothers were keeping an eye on his transactions, probably hoping to catch him with a jar of evidence, so they could confiscate it, either to resell or to consume.

He wasn't really worried that they'd run him in or force him to reveal the whereabouts of Dayman's still. It was in their best interests, after all, to allow a few stills go to on operating, so they had something to confiscate. The only thing likely to change that was for federal revenue agents to come nosing around.

Thad doubted that would happen. It wasn't like it was during Prohibition, when the county was a major supplier of bootleg whiskey for the speakeasies in Kansas City and Tulsa. It was all small-time now. No one was getting rich. Making liquor was just a way for a fellow to earn enough to live on, in the absence of any real jobs.

If the law was watching him that closely, it wasn't wise to go on doing business as he had been, bringing the customer to the product. All Pearly or Charley had to do then was follow the tourister's car. Better to hide the jar close to home, find himself a customer, and arrange to meet him at some out of the way place to complete the sale.

He'd have to conceal it soon. It wouldn't do to carry the jar through town. The derelict Model T seemed as good a place as any. He'd left his brogans there a dozen times, and no one had disturbed them.

Thad retrieved his shoes, then tucked the Mason jar under the battered front seat of the automobile and closed the door softly.

It was getting late in the day. Momma would be off work by now, and would fret if he didn't turn up for supper. He didn't want her questioning him again about where he'd been. The transaction could wait until tomorrow. He slipped on his brogans and went home.

Momma was in the kitchen, cutting mold off a loaf of bread the café had let her have. She looked up, smiling wearily, then glanced down at his empty hands. "Didn't you bring nothing?"

Thad mentally kicked himself. With all the corn liquor business, he'd completely forgotten about the need to bring home meat for the table. "I didn't see much of anything," he said. "And what I did see I couldn't get close to. I really need me a gun, Momma. I could get us a deer, then, or a wild hog, something that would make more than just one meal."

"Well, now, if'n I had enough for a gun, I'd have enough to buy food, wouldn't I?"

"Clem Cordell has a twenty-two he says he'll sell me for four dollars."

"You can't very well kill a deer with a twenty-two. Besides, four dollars is just about three dollars and fifty cents more than we got."

"I thought you said you'd get some tips."

"Oh, I did. All of thirty cents. I used it to buy canned milk and oleo. The café don't pay me for four more days yet."

"Ain't we got nothing?"

"This bread, enough flour to make poor man's gravy, I guess. Oh, and a couple slices of pie nobody wanted cause they was so tore up."

"What kind of pie?"

"Apple."

"Well, then," said Thad cheerfully. "What more could a body want? 'A loaf of bread beneath the bough, a slice of apple pie, and thou beside me, singing in the wilderness.'"

Momma laughed. "What kind of moonshine is that?"

"It's a poem Mrs. Mitchell had us learn for English class. Only it was a flask of wine, not apple pie. But I reckon I like the pie better. Let's eat."

"All right," Momma said. "But don't expect me to do no singing."

7

Thad rose even earlier than usual in the morning, meaning to bring home a string of fish to make up for yesterday. He had a thick slice of bread spread with oleo by way of breakfast, and he and Dauncey were well out of town before the sun rose.

The short night hadn't done much to alleviate the heat and humidity in the air. If a fellow wanted to catch more than one or two fish in this kind of weather, he had to know where to look. Thad knew just where.

At the rear of the Christensen estate was a private pond stocked with some sizable bass. He also knew where there was a gap between the fence and the ground, just large enough for him to squeeze through the last time he'd tried.

Unfortunately that had been last summer, and he'd grown considerably since then. He let Dauncey go under the fence first. The hound pawed at the dirt, and dug away enough of it so Thad could wriggle through on his back if he pushed up on the wire with his hands.

The pond was in the middle of an open field, with no trees to put between him and the big brick Christensen house. But it wasn't likely anyone would be up and around yet to see him. Even so, he kept as low to the ground as he could.

Thad always carried with him a length or two of fishing line in the bib pocket of his overalls and several hooks stuck in an old bottle cork. He tied one hook on the end of the line and threaded the other end through a hole in the cork, which would serve as his bobber. Then he turned up some of the large, flat rocks nearby until he uncovered several earthworms, which he stuffed in his pocket, along with enough dirt to keep them happy.

He made himself a stringer out of another length of fishing line tied to a stick. Inside an hour he had four largemouth bass on the stringer, and five sunfish. He glanced up at the sun. It must be close to seven o'clock. No sense pressing his luck.

As he was standing up, dumping the dirt from his pocket, he spotted a man striding across the field from the house, a spaniel dog trotting at his side. It was hard to be sure at this distance, but it looked as if the man had a shotgun cradled in one arm. "Lordy, Dauncey!" Thad breathed. "Let's clear out of here!"

He snatched up the stringer and made a dash for the fence, keeping bent over, to offer a smaller target. He heard the man holler after him, and the dog began barking. Thad dropped the fish next to the fence, threw himself on his back, and squirmed under the wire. As he turned and reached his arm back through to snag the stringer, he saw the spaniel come tearing around the edge of the pond, barking furiously.

Dauncey turned to face the dog, and bellowed back at him. The spaniel pulled up short and began dashing back and forth, making an awful racket.

"Dauncey!" Thad yelled over all the barking. "Durn you, Dauncey, come on!" But the hound was too busy dealing with the spaniel to respond. Thad glanced toward the pond. The dog's owner was still coming at a brisk walk, and he appeared to be slipping shells into the shotgun as he came.

"Dauncey!" Thad shouted, more frantically. The dog pricked up his ears, so Thad knew he'd heard, but still he wouldn't back down. Desperate, Thad picked up the nearest rock and, sticking his arm under the fence, flung it at Dauncey. It struck the hound square in the hind end, making him yelp in surprise and turn to give Thad a reproachful look.

"You come on, now!" Thad ordered, and this time Dauncey obeyed. As they sprinted down the hill toward a line of trees, Thad heard the blast of the shotgun, and flinched. It could be that the man was only firing into the air to scare them, but Thad didn't care to wait around in order to be sure.

✻   ✻   ✻

As soon as he got home, he put the four bass into a bucket of cold water to keep them fresh. Then he cleaned the sunfish and Momma dipped them in cornmeal and fried them up for an early lunch.

"How'd you manage to catch so many?" Momma wanted to know.

"Well, being as it was so early, I figure they was still half asleep and not thinking real clear."

"Where'd you go?"

"Up toward Decker Camp."

"I'd of thought the water was too shallow on the Little Sugar, as dry as it is."

"Well, there's this deep hole up there. Not many folks know about it." She seemed satisfied with his story. Still, it would be a good idea not to let her see the four bass. Though she didn't know much about fishing, she might be aware that there were no largemouth bass in the Little Sugar—or the Elk River, either, so far as he knew.

Right after lunch he carried the bucket full of bass down to the Elk River Resort. Dauncey trailed after him. Unlike most dogs, Dauncey didn't waste much time sniffing bushes and light poles and leaving his mark. It was as if he just didn't care what other dogs had been there before him.

Two touristers were fishing off the wooden dock that belonged to the resort. The men were as different as Mutt and Jeff in the funny papers. It was as if someone had put them there side by side deliberately, in order to graphically illustrate the term "opposites."

One was a fat older fellow in an undershirt and shorts that revealed pale, puffy legs tattooed with dark veins.

His battered canvas hat sported a wide hatband stuck full of hooks and artificial flies. His worn steel pole had been spliced together, and the reel was rusty.

The other man, who looked to be in his late thirties, was a head taller and fifty pounds lighter. His khaki trousers and his tan fedora hat were both smooth and spotless. The sleeves of his white shirt, which were rolled halfway up his forearms, looked even whiter against his tanned skin. His reel and bamboo rod looked as if they'd come in the mail from Sears, Roebuck a day or two previous.

Thad put the old fellow down as a lifelong fisherman who would be insulted at the idea of feasting on any fish he hadn't caught himself. The tall man looked to him more like a fair-weather fisherman who would lose patience quickly and be ready to settle for fish from a bucket.

Dauncey hung back while Thad approached the men. The old tourister ignored him. The younger one nodded cordially and said, "That's a fine-looking hound. Does he belong to you?"

"He don't belong to me," Thad said. "But he lives at our house."

The man smiled, showing white, even teeth. "A good distinction to make."

"You catching anything?"

"Not yet. But it's still early."

"Early?" grumbled the old fellow. "I've been out here for two hours and haven't had a nibble. The brochure the resort sent me said this river was full of fish."

"So it is," said Thad. "That's on account of they so seldom get caught."

The tall man laughed and looked down at the bass in the bucket. "It doesn't look as if you had much trouble."

"Oh, I caught lots more than this. This is just the extras that we got no use for."

The old man peered curiously into the bucket. "What kind are those?"

"Largemouth bass."

"Bass, eh? I suppose you want a lot for them."

"Ten cents apiece."

"Sold. On one condition. You don't tell my wife where they came from."

"You ain't going to lie to her?" Thad said in mock dismay.

"No. I just plan to withhold certain information."

Thad started to hand over the bucket, but the tall man put out a hand to stop him. "Just a minute. I'll give you fifteen cents apiece for those."

The old man scowled at him. "Now, see here. He already said he'd sell them to me for ten."

"Well, I'm making a higher bid."

"I didn't know this was going to be an auction. All right. I'll make it twenty cents."

"Twenty-five," said the tall man.

"Thirty, and that's my final offer."

The tall man grinned and shook his head. "Too rich for my blood. I guess I'll have to catch my own."

"Ha!" said the old man triumphantly. While he dug out the money, Thad rigged up a stringer and slid the fish onto it.

"There. That'll look more regular."

The old man went off, smiling smugly, to exhibit his

catch. Thad said to the tall man, "I reckon you didn't want them fish at all, did you?"

"Of course I did," the man said, innocently.

"No, you didn't. You was just seeing to it that I got more money for them."

The man shrugged. "I believe a man should get a fair wage for his work."

"It wasn't much work. I didn't take me but about an hour to catch them."

The man raised his eyebrows. "An hour? What do you use? Magic?"

"Just plain old earthworms."

The man reeled in his line. His bait was untouched. "That's what I've been using, and the only thing I get is drowned worms."

"Well, you got to know where to go."

The man set down his rod and regarded Thad thoughtfully. "I don't suppose you'd care to show me. I'd make it worth your while. Say, five dollars?"

Thad blinked in surprise. Five dollars was a sight of money. With that, and the dollar twenty he'd made from the fish, he could pay Dayman for the lost liquor and still have over half of what he needed to buy Clem's twenty-two.

But of course it would hardly do to let this tourister in on the location of his secret fishing hole, considering that it and the Christensens' private pond were one and the same.

He could, he supposed, lead the man to some other fishing spot and claim that it was where he'd taken the bass. But that would be deceitful. Making up a bit of moonshine for Momma so she wouldn't fret was one thing. Striking a bargain with a person and then not living up to it was a whole other thing.

"No sir," Thad said, regretfully. "I can't do that."

The man didn't react with anger, as touristers so often did when they didn't get what they wanted when they wanted it. Instead he smiled wryly. "I thought not. If you want to know the truth, I'd have been disappointed if you'd said yes. There ought to be some things in this world that aren't for sale."

"There's lots better places on the Elk River to fish than this, though, and I wouldn't mind showing you one of them, at no charge."

"Are they in walking distance?"

"Well, some are. But the best spot I know of is down past Noel, at Cedar Bluff. Most of the touristers fish out of boats, and don't none of them generally float down that far."

"Is there a road that takes you there?"

"Yes sir."

He picked up his bamboo pole. "Let's go, then."

Thad whistled for Dauncey, who was splashing around in the water, chasing minnows. As they headed for the tourist cabins, the man said, "By the say, my name is Harlan. Harlan James."

"Thad McCune." Thad shook his hand. "You any relation to Jesse?"

Harlan laughed. "Not that I know of. I'm not from Missouri."

"I figured that much, from the way you talk."

"Oh? What did I say that gave me away?"

"It's more a case of what you don't say. Folks around here ain't very refined in their speech."

"Well, I've always felt it's what you say that matters, not how you say it." He laid his fishing pole in the back of a green Dodge convertible of recent vintage. There was another pole there already, as new-looking as the first, plus an oak fishing creel and a pair of hip boots.

"You sure got a lot of nice fishing gear."

"More than I need, really. When I was a boy, I made do with a hickory stick and some twine."

"I often do without the stick," Thad said.

"Well, we'll see how you like using a twenty-dollar rod and reel."

Thad whistled. "Twenty dollars? What do you do for a living? Rob banks?"

"I told you, I'm not related to Jesse James. Actually, I'm in the tobacco business." He gestured at the automobile. "Go ahead; get in."

"I can't leave Dauncey here."

"He can ride in the back. There's plenty of room."

"You sure? I wouldn't like for him to get your upholstery wet and dirty."

"It's leather. It'll clean."

Thad and Dauncey climbed in. When Harlan started up the Dodge, Thad could scarcely tell, it ran so smooth and quiet. They cruised up Main Street, passing Clem Cordell, who stared open-mouthed as Thad waved to him.

"I'll buy some food for us," Harlan said, "and then we'll run by your house so you can make sure it's all right with your parents to go."

"There's just my momma, and she'll be at the café. She

54

wouldn't mind making up some sandwiches for us, I expect."

Momma seemed surprised and gratified that Thad had seen fit to tell her where he was off to for a change. Thad didn't tell her that it had been Harlan's idea. When Harlan introduced himself, Momma acted oddly embarrassed and at a loss for words, and seemed relieved to retreat to the kitchen and make the sandwiches.

"I put you in each an apple and a bottle of soda pop," she said as she handed the poke to Thad.

"That sounds perfect," Harlan said. "How much do I owe you?"

She shrugged. "Thirty cents be all right?"

"No," Harlan said. "It would be highway robbery." She looked startled and flustered until he added, "I won't give you a cent less than fifty."

Momma smiled slyly. "I won't argue with you." Her face looked slightly flushed, and Thad suspected it wasn't just from the heat.

"Good. I'll have your boy back by dinnertime."

"He means supper," Thad explained. "Folks from the city talk different."

"I knew that," Momma said.

As they got into the automobile, Harlan said, "She certainly looks young to be the mother of a strapping fellow like you."

"I ain't but thirteen," Thad said. "Folks always take me for older because I'm tall."

"What happened to your father?"

"He was killed. In the line of duty." Thad launched into the lie without so much as a hesitation.

Harlan glanced over at him. "Oh? What was he, a law officer?"

"Yes sir. He was the sheriff of this county. It was bank robbers done it. My daddy managed to do the lot of them in, though, before he went down. He was a crack shot. The bank got back every cent of the money, too."

"I see," said Harlan soberly. "These robbers—they weren't by any chance the James gang, were they?

Thad gave him a surprised look. "Of course not. Jesse James has been dead for fifty years or more."

"Oh, I don't know. I've heard people say old Jesse just staged his death, and it really still alive somewhere."

Thad snorted derisively. "He'd have to be about a hundred years old."

"Well, you know, just in the few weeks I've been in the Ozarks, I've heard at least ten different stories about Jesse and how he robbed this bank, or hid out in that cave, or gave money to a widow who lived in a particular house. For Jesse to have done everything and been every place that people claim, he'd have to be at least a hundred."

"I reckon," Thad said.

Harlan drove in silence for a minute, then said, "Why do people tell stories like that, do you suppose? Do you think they really believe them?"

"Could be. Or maybe they just tell them because a good tale is a sight more interesting and satisfying that what really happened."

Harlan nodded. "That's about the way I had it figured, too."

8

The fishing wasn't much better at Cedar Bluff than it had been at the resort. "I reckon it's the heat," Thad said. "Fish like to hide in the deep spots when it's this hot."

Harlan lay back against the sycamore tree in whose shade they sat. "That's all right. There's more to fishing than just catching fish."

Thad grinned. "That's so. If'n all a body wants is a lot of fish, there's better ways to go about it." He looked down at the twenty-dollar pole, which was light as an elder stick in his hand. "And cheaper, too."

"Dynamiting, you mean?"

"Well, I've heard of folks doing that, but it never did seem like playing fair to me."

"It's also illegal."

"I ain't surprised. I don't know whether or not goosing is legal, but I do know it works."

Harlan laughed. "Goosing?"

"Yes sir. How it works is, you wait until just after a big rain, when the water's good and muddy, then you get you a johnboat, and you pull up alongside a patch of weeds. You take you a pole and kind of stir up the water next to the boat. The fish, they get all confused because they can't see, on account of the mud, and they commence jumping up, and a good number of them will jump right into the boat."

Harlan nodded, but his expression was skeptical and amused. "I'll just bet this—what did you call it? Goosing? I'll just bet it was something that Jesse James was an expert at."

Thad asked indignantly, "Are you saying you don't believe me?"

"No, no! I'd just like to see this wonderful technique in action, that's all."

"Well, it's like I said, the water has to be real muddy. If'n it ever decides to rain, I'll sure enough give you a demonstration. Of course, if'n you want to keep the fish, I'll be obliged to charge you two bits apiece."

"What? You were going to let Mr. Chaney have his for ten."

"Well, but that was before you went and convinced me that it wasn't a fair wage."

Harlan sighed. "All right. It'll be worth two bits apiece to see fish volunteer to jump into a boat. Of course, I can't guarantee that I'll still be here by the time it rains again."

"Oh? How long did you have in mind to stay?"

"That depends."

"On what?"

Harlan took his time replying. He got to his feet and reeled in his line, the reel making a soft whirring sound. Then he threaded a new worm onto the hook and made an effortless cast to the far side of the river, in the shadow of the bluff. As he sat back down, he said, "Can you keep a secret?"

"Sure."

"Well, I don't want this to get out, but I'm not just here on vacation. I'm looking at the land around here with an eye to whether or not it's suitable for growing tobacco. If it turns out that it is, it could be a real boost to the county's economy."

"Why don't you want folks to know?"

"If they thought a big tobacco company was interested in buying up their land, they'd demand a much higher price, and the cost of the land is one of the big factors that determines whether or not the whole plan is feasible."

Thad nodded. "You can count on me not to say nothing."

"If you don't say nothing," Harlan pointed out, straight-faced, "that means you will say something."

"All right, then, I won't say ary thing. Is that better?

"I reckon," Harlan said.

They changed the location of their lines several times without any results. Thad began to feel foolish for having claimed that this was a good fishing spot.

Sometime after noon they broke out the sandwiches. Thad's momma had wisely given them bacon, lettuce and tomato on buttered bread. Cheese or lunchmeat would have gone bad in this heat. Thad tossed the last of his sandwich to Dauncey, and retrieved the bottles of soda pop from the river, where they had been keeping relatively cool.

Harlan used the edge of his expensive fishing reel as a bottle opener. Thad was taken aback. If he ever had himself a twenty-dollar rod and reel, or new and costly clothing, or a fancy automobile with leather seats, he felt sure he'd be a lot more careful with them than Harlan seemed to be. Of course it was highly unlikely that he'd ever have the opportunity to find out. Chances were he'd go on making do with homemade fishing gear and patched clothing and getting around on foot for a long time to come.

Harlan gulped down half a bottle of cream soda. "That hits the spot," he said. "I do wish a man could buy something with more moxie, though. If I had known this was a dry county, I would have brought a supply with me."

"I reckon you mean whiskey."

"You reckon right. This is a dry county, isn't it?"

"Strictly speaking. But you know, whiskey is a lot like fish."

"Meaning you have to know where to look for it? I don't suppose there's any chance that you'd be privy to that sort of information?"

"I'd say there's a pretty good chance."

"Really? I mean, no offense, but you also said you knew where there was some good fishing."

As if it had been waiting for just that moment, Thad's reel sang out. Thad made a dive for the pole, which was slithering toward the water.

"Put the drag on!" Harlan yelled over the whining of the reel.

"The what?"

"The button on the left side; push it down!"

When Thad pushed on the button, the rate at which the line was flying off the reel slowed, and he felt the pull of the fish for the first time.

"Keep the tip of the rod up, so you have some play," Harlan instructed him.

Thad did so, and the rod bent like a bow. "God durn! It must be a big one!"

"That's all right. That pole has twenty-five pound test line."

Thad gave him an alarmed look. "Twenty-five pounds?

The mud cats in this river can run upwards of fifty pounds."

Harlan laughed, "Fifty pound catfish? Who catches them? Jesse James?"

"That ain't no moonshine, I swear! Why, just last month Lafe Butterworth come home with a seventy pounder. Folks say a few years back some tourister landed a catfish weighed more than he did."

"Yes, well, you're not going to land this one if you don't stop talking and start pulling him in."

Thad grunted as he dragged on the pole and wound a foot or two of line onto the reel. "I ain't sure but what he's the one going to pull me in. Maybe you better take him, Harlan. I don't care to lose a twenty-dollar fishing pole."

"No, he's yours. You can do it. You just have to hang on until you tire him out. First let him run with it a little, then reel him in a little. Just be sure you keep the line taut. And try to keep him in the middle of the river, so he can't snag the line on something."

"I'll try," Thad said, between clenched teeth.

The presumed catfish showed no sign of tiring any time soon. Thad's arms, however, did. Harlan went to the car and returned with the oak creel. "Here, sit on this and brace your feet. That'll take some of the strain off."

"I wouldn't like to break your fishing basket."

"You won't and it doesn't matter if you do, because if that fellow is as big as I think he is, he won't fit in there anyway—not in one piece."

Sitting down did help some, but not much. After fighting the fish for what had to be half an hour, and dragging him a total of about five feet closer, Thad had begun to fear that he might share Dayman's fate, or go him one better by losing both arms.

Though his hands had long since gone numb, the muscles in his shoulders and back were on fire. "I can't hold him much longer, Harlan!" he groaned. "I just can't!"

"If you keep saying you can't, then you surely won't. The only way you'll ever do it is to keep telling yourself you can."

"But how can I tell myself I can if'n I know I can't?"

"Lie to yourself!"

"I can hold him," Thad said, gritting his teeth. "I can do it."

The fish gave a sudden jerk, and the line went whizzing through the eyelets of the rod. Thad lost his grip on the crank of the reel and it spun around like a propellor, thumping painfully against his fingers. Desperate, he jammed his left thumb against the fast-dwindling spool of line. The friction burned his skin, making him cry out. But the pressure of his thumb slowed things down enough so he could get hold of the crank again. He wound it furiously with his aching fingers, trying to take up some of the line he'd lost.

The line on the reel was turning red, and Thad realized that the friction had worn the skin right off his thumb. He'd scarcely noticed the pain; it had to compete with the pain in his other hand, and in his back and shoulders. "You done it now, fish!" he yelled. "You got me riled, and now I'm going to drag your spiny butt out of that river and beat your bull head in with a rock and fry you up for supper!"

"That's the spirit!" said Harlan, and clapped him on his aching back.

Though he was as exhausted as he'd ever been, the fish was apparently more so. It was still thrashing, but its struggles were growing weaker. When Thad got it to within two feet of the shore, Dauncey lunged into the water, barking as if he meant to tear the fish to pieces. "No, Dauncey!" Thad yelled.

Harlan waded out with a net in his hand and scooped up the fish—or at least most of it. It was, as they'd figured, a catfish, and one of such size that a foot of it hung over the edge of the net.

Thad grabbed up a sizable rock, staggered to Harlan's side, and with the last of his strength, pounded the catfish's head as he had promised. "Watch out for the spines," he managed to say, and then he fell backward on the gravel. He lay there a long while, feeling as if he were the one who'd been hooked and landed and clobbered with a rock.

After a time he heard Harlan say, in a tone of disappointment, "Well, I wish I could say he was a fifty-pounder."

Thad sat up, wincing and flexing his stiff shoulder muscles. Harlan had the catfish hanging by its gills from a portable scale. The fish was so enormous that Harlan had to hold the scale practically at shoulder height to keep the catch from dragging on the ground. "Shoot," Thad said. "He felt like a ton. How much *does* he weigh?"

Harlan shrugged. "I can't tell."

"Why not?"

Harlan's sober face broke into a grin. "Because. My scale only goes up to forty pounds."

Thad's eyes widened. "So he could be *more* than fifty?"

"He could be a hundred, just like Jesse James."

I reckon we could have him weighed down to the feed store," Thad said. Then he considered a moment and shook his head. "No, on second thought I don't believe I'll do that. It'll make a better story if we don't never know for certain." He glanced at Harlan's drenched, muddy pant legs, and laughed. "You surely made a mess of your shoes and your britches."

"It was worth it."

"Yeah," Thad said, grinning wearily. "It was. I'm obliged to you."

Harlan had taken a rubber raincoat from the trunk of the car and was carefully wrapping the catfish in it. "I didn't contribute anything except the pole and the net."

"That's a lot. I couldn't never have brought him in with just an old hickory pole."

"Maybe. Even so, you did all the work. You should be proud."

"I am. But if'n you hadn't made me keep at it, I'd of given up."

"I doubt it." Harlan wrestled the wrapped fish into the trunk. "Anyway, this calls for a celebration. Is there any chance you could introduce me to one of your local distillers?"

"No, sir. But I could let you meet about a quart of his product."

"Good man. Lead me to it."

"You know," Thad said as they drove back to town, "I don't reckon me and Momma will be able to use more than half that lunker before it spoils, even allowing for what Dauncey will eat. We'd be obliged if'n you'd come to supper."

Harlan gazed at him thoughtfully a moment, and then nodded. "All right. I'd be willing to bet your mother is a fine cook."

"You'd win that bet, too. One thing, though. You can't let on about the corn liquor. Momma don't know nothing about that, and I'd like for it to stay that way. I don't drink none of it, you understand. I just collect the money for it."

"I understand." Harlan thrust out his hand. "You keep my secret, and I'll keep yours. Deal?"

"Deal." Thad put his hand into Harlan's grasp, and gasped as it sent a jolt of pain through his bruised fingers.

On the way to the house they stopped at the rusty, wheel-less Model T that served as Thad's storage shed. He climbed stiffly out of the convertible, opened the door of the Ford, and stuck an arm under the front seat.

The only thing he found there was a broken spring that raked his forearm. The Mason jar of corn liquor was gone.

Thad laid his head down and examined the floor beneath the seat, hoping the jar had somehow gotten pushed into some cranny. But there wasn't a sign of it. He got slowly to his feet, feeling dazed. He couldn't possibly afford to lose another jar of Dayman's whisky and another four dollars. But it looked as if he had.

He gave the side of the Model T a spiteful kick with his bare foot, then wished he hadn't. Crouching, he examined the dusty road next to the car. Mixed in with his own bare footprints were the impressions of a pair of hobnail boots—the same sort of boots that were worn by half the men in McDonald County.

With a sigh of defeat, he returned to Harlan's car and slumped in the seat.

"What's wrong?" Harlan asked.

"It ain't there. Somebody up and took it."

Harlan put a hand on his shoulder. "It doesn't matter. I can pick some up in Springfield. Or you can visit your supplier and get another bottle."

"I don't know if'n I can or not. That's the second jar of it I lost in three days. He ain't likely to trust me with another one."

"It wasn't your fault if they were stolen. Would it help if I went along and vouched for you?"

"No." He didn't like to sound rude that way. He knew Harlan meant well, and he wanted to explain how it wouldn't do to let anybody in on the whereabouts of Dayman's still, no matter who. But he figured the less he said, the better.

As they drove up Dog Hollow Road, Thad spotted Pearly Rickett's old Chevrolet pulled up in front of his house. "God durn it," he muttered. It seemed as if some folks were bound and determined to take all the pleasure out of a day that had been shaping up unusually good. "You can let me and Dauncey out here. I reckon you'll want to go and clean up anyway, before supper."

Harlan gave him a curious look but said, "All right."

As Thad and Dauncey climbed out, he added, "I don't have to come at all, if it's a problem. We can make it another day."

"No, it'll be okay. I just need to . . . I just need to tell Momma so she can straighten up some. You know how women are."

"More or less. I'm not married, but I do have a mother."

"And a daddy, too?"

"And a daddy, too. And no, his name isn't Jesse, or even Frank. It's Harlan James, Senior."

"So you're named after him. My Momma named me after her granddaddy. Oh. I reckon I ought to tell you, this ain't our house here." Thad started to point up the street to his real house, then hesitated. He'd never given much thought before to how their house looked, but at the moment he found himself seeing it as it must look to someone like Harlan, and he felt an unaccustomed twinge of something like shame.

The house certainly wasn't much to look at. It gave the impression of being assembled from parts taken from several different houses, none of them any great shakes, and fastened together any which way, and not very securely at that. Like almost all the houses in Pineville, it had a porch, but just barely; it looked as if it might part company with the rest of the building at any time.

Instead of shingles or corrugated zinc, the roof was covered with ragged black tar paper. The siding was not stone or even clapboard, but a thick, tar paperlike material that he suspected was meant to resemble brick but didn't.

Thad considered telling Harlan that some other house was his—the Kinsley place, for example, with its brick walls and stone porch and white wooden columns, or even Clem Cordell's house, which was at least freshly painted.

But he'd asked Harlan to dinner and he doubted that he could talk Clem and his folks into trading residences, even for a couple of hours. He had to either admit to living where he did or back out on the dinner invitation.

"Ours is the little bitty place four houses up," he said. "It ain't nothing fancy."

"I can get fancy at home," Harlan said. "But I can't get home-cooked catfish."

"Well, see you in an hour, then. Don't you forget to bring my fish."

Harlan laughed and waved as he pulled away. "I won't."

Thad approached the house quietly, meaning to listen at the back door to see if he could make out what the nature of Pearly Rickett's visit was. Had he come courting again? Or was he here on business, possibly something to do with Thad's early-morning fishing expedition to the Christensen estate?

Before he reached the house, the front door opened and Pearly backed out onto the porch with his hat in his hands. Thad stepped behind a sycamore tree, and motioned Dauncey to sit next to him.

"You take care, now, Jo," the deputy was saying. So he had graduated to "Jo" now, not "Miz McCune." "Don't let them work you too hard down to that café. They don't make you peel potatoes, do they? When I was in the navy, that was the thing I hated the most. I didn't mind blowing up them German U-boats, but it surely did gravel me, having to peel potatoes."

"I don't do much in the kitchen," he heard his momma say from indoors. "But I wouldn't complain if'n I did. We could use the money."

"Well, now," said Pearly, sounding as if he meant to be charming but hadn't got the hang of it, "if'n you'd just let some good man take care of you, you wouldn't have to fret none."

Momma laughed. "Why, that would just give me one more thing to fret about. Besides, all the good men are married off."

"Well, I don't know about that." Pearly sounded deflated and hurt. He stood there awkwardly a moment, then said, "Well, good evening." As he shuffled backward, his foot caught on one of the uneven boards of the porch and he came very near to tumbling down the steps. Thad had to clamp his hand over his mouth to keep from exploding with laughter. Pearly recovered and stomped off to his automobile.

Thad found Momma in the kitchen, about to open a can of pork and beans. "Wait!" he said.

She jumped about a foot. "My lord, Thad, you about gave me a coronary."

"I didn't want you opening that can. I got a surprise for supper."

She put down the can opener and smiled at him quizzically. "Well? Where is it?"

"It's coming. Oh, and we got company coming, too."

"Company? Who?"

"Harlan James. The fellow you met this morning."

"Oh, Thad! You should have told me!"

"I just did."

"But the place is a mess!"

"Well, he ain't coming for an hour yet. I'll help you straighten up."

"I'll have to change my clothes, too, and fix my hair," she fretted.

"You go on ahead, and I'll sweep up some," Thad said. She disappeared into the bedroom. As he swept the kitchen floor, he called, "What did *he* want?"

"Who?"

"Moss-mouth."

"Thad!" his momma chided, but he thought he heard her stifle a laugh. "He brought me a present."

Thad rolled his eyes. "I told you he was aiming to court you."

"Not that kind of a present. Look behind the stove."

Puzzled, Thad peered in back of the wood cookstove. In a cardboard box something was curled up on a blanket. When he crouched down and picked it up, it yelped and squirmed. "Well, I'll be," Thad said. It was a small, frightened beagle puppy. Thad held it to his chest, where it buried its head in the pocket of his overalls. "What made him think you'd want another dog?"

"It wasn't a case of me wanting him so much as of him needing a home." Momma emerged from the bedroom wearing a clean print dress and brushing her short, dark hair. "His momma got a case of the rabies, and the owner called in Pearly to put her down. The momma was so far gone, she'd killed two of her pups. this one had hid behind the woodpile. The owner didn't want him; he was afraid the pup would come down with rabies, too. But it don't seem likely. There's nary a mark on him."

"I reckon Pearly has heard what a soft touch you are."

She gave a slight, shamefaced shrug. "I reckon he has." It was a long-standing joke between them, her tendency to take in every sort of stray, from injured rabbits to worm-ridden cats.

"Poor little guy," Thad said, stroking the puppy's fur. "How could his momma do that, you reckon? Kill her own babies that way?"

"She was out of her head from the rabies. I expect she didn't have no idea what she was even doing. By the way, you got to shut Dauncey up in the shed. He can't be running loose, with the rabies going around like it is."

"Momma, you know how Dauncey hates being shut up. Couldn't we just keep him in the house? He ain't no trouble."

"No. It'd be too easy for him to get out through one of the screen doors. We can't take no chances. Pearly says there's been six reports of rabies just this week. We can't take no chances. Go on, now."

Thad scowled, but did as she said. As he pushed open the screen door, he noticed that the torn, rusted screen had been mended with bright new material. "Who done this?"

"Pearly Rickett."

"I told you and him I'd take care of it."

"It couldn't wait. The way it was, the puppy could of squirmed right out through it."

"So you aim to keep both him and Dauncey locked up like thieves?"

"It's for their own good," Momma started to say, but the slamming of the screen door cut her off.

As Thad expected, Dauncey wasn't at all happy about being shut up in the shed, and began to whine almost at once. "I'm really sorry, boy," Thad told him. "If'n you be good, I'll bring you some fried catfish and hush puppies later." The hound quieted down then.

Thad turned to go in and saw Clem Cordell coming up the street. Clem beckoned to him. "Say, I just seen Willa Houseman. She says to tell you to meet her at Minnie Brewer's tomorrow at six o'clock."

"What for?"

"I guess they're going to see a moving picture over to Anderson. Some Western picture with Randolph Scott. Wish she'd asked me. I like Westerns, don't you?"

"I can't say, since I never seen one."

Clem laughed. "Wait till you see. The guns in them things can shoot sixty-seven times without ever reloading. All except for the bad guy's gun. See, the good guy, he always counts up how many times the bad guy shoots, then he steps out of hiding. When the bad guy realizes he's got no bullets left he always throws his gun at the good guy."

Thad frowned in puzzlement. "If'n you know just how a picture is going to turn out, what's the use in sitting though it?"

Clem seemed stumped for a moment, then said, "Well, it wouldn't do for the good guy to get shot, now, would it?"

"I don't know. It just sounds to me like moving pictures wouldn't be nearly as interesting as real life. In real life you never know how things are going to turn out."

"And that's just what I don't like about it. Say, speaking

of guns—you give any thought to what I said about that twenty-two of mine?"

"Does it shoot sixty-seven times without reloading?"

"No."

"Then it can't be much account. I got to go in now and help my momma. We're having company for supper."

"Who's that?"

"The tourister you seen me in the automobile with."

"No fooling? That was some vehicle. Wish I had me an automobile like that. How much you reckon that set him back?"

"He told me he paid over a thousand dollars for it, " Thad lied. "You ought to see his fishing gear. He's got a pole and a reel that cost him fifty dollars."

"Go on!" Clem said.

"In fact he's got two of them, and he let me borrow one. I caught me a big mud cat with it, and I do mean big. This feller has a weighing scale that goes up to eighty pounds, and my fish broke it."

Clem whistled. "I never did see no fish that big."

"You can't see this one, either. We already cleaned it and cut it up. I'll show you the head sometime. Right now I got to go. Thanks for giving me Willa's message."

"That's all right. If'n you decide not to go, tell her I'll be glad to take your place. Her folks like me better than they do you, anyway."

"Yeah," Thad replied, "and some people like raw fish eggs. There ain't no accounting for taste."

10

Around six o'clock the green Dodge pulled up in front of the house and Harlan James came carrying an aluminum ice chest up onto the porch. Thad opened the lopsided screen door for him. Once again he was painfully aware of what bad shape the house was in. "Mind them rotten boards, now."

"Thanks." Harlan winced and shifted the weight of the ice chest. "As heavy as this is, it just might send me crashing through."

"Is that my fish in there?"

Harlan set the chest on the kitchen floor. "What's left of it."

"What do you mean?"

"Take a look." Harlan opened the lid of the chest. Inside laid out on a block of ice, was the big cat—minus the head and tail and the fins and bones, and all cut up into pan-size fillets.

"You done all that?"

"No, the butcher down at the grocery store did. I thought that after all you went through to catch it, you shouldn't have to clean it, too."

Momma emerged from the bedroom, wearing lipstick and a tentative smile. "Hello," she said.

"Good evening." Harlan pulled off his fedora with one hand and with the other took momma's hand. "I almost didn't recognize you, you look so different from the way you did this afternoon."

"That's just what I was about to say to this fish," Thad put in, and they all laughed.

Harlan worked right alongside Momma, stirring the hush puppy batter for her, and rolling the catfish fillets in flour before she slid them into the hot oil in the skillet. Thad sat holding the beagle puppy and feeling a little left out. Out in the shed, Dauncey began barking and whining. He feels left out, too, Thad thought.

"Is that Dauncey complaining?" Harlan asked.

Momma nodded and wiped her forehead, leaving a track of flour. "We got to keep him shut up. There's rabies going around."

"It don't seem necessary to me," Thad said. "Dauncey's smart enough not to tangle with no animal that's acting crazy."

"Maybe he is and maybe he ain't," Momma said. "It ain't worth taking a chance."

"I'd have to agree with your mother," Harlan said. "It's too risky. My understanding is that if a dog catches rabies, there's no treatment for it."

Who asked you? Thad almost said, but held his tongue. He liked Harlan, and didn't care to put him off. It was just that he'd sounded an awful lot like a second parent just then. Thad had often thought about what it would be like to have a daddy around, but had failed to consider that it would mean another person telling him what he ought and ought not to do. Still, if a body was bound to have a daddy, Thad reckoned, he could do a lot worse than Harlan James. Pearly Rickett, for example.

The supper was neither quite a failure nor quite a

success. Though the catfish was excellent, the conversation left a lot to be desired. It consisted mostly of Momma making apologies for things—the rickety chairs, the chipped plates, the worn oilcloth on the table—and Harlan assuring her that it didn't matter to him. When Momma apologized for not having anything more suitable to drink than well water—they had finished off Pearly Rickett's coffee that morning—Harlan turned and gave Thad a wink, and Thad grinned ruefully, knowing Harlan was thinking about the corn liquor.

At one point the conversation threatened to die altogether, and Thad revived it by saying, "Do you get to see many moving pictures where you come from?"

Harlan nodded and swallowed his mouthful of fish. "There are dozens of movie theaters in Washington."

"You like Westerns?"

"That depends on the Western, and who the actors are."

"I got a chance to go see a Randoph Scott picture. You reckon I'll like it?"

"Randolph Scott is one of my favorites."

"Who are you going with?" Momma asked.

"Minnie Brewer and her folks." Thad deliberately failed to mention Willa. Momma knew well enough that the Housemans didn't want Thad associating with her.

Momma raised her eyebrows and smiled "I didn't know you and Minnie Brewer were an item."

"We ain't an *item*. She asked me to go to a moving picture, that's all."

"Well, I hate to say it, but I'm glad you've taken up with someone besides Willa Houseman. Minnie's a good girl, from a good family. Her momma and me have been friends forever. It ain't that I don't like Willa, you know that. I like her fine. But I know how her folks feel about me."

"It ain't you they object to, Momma. It's me. They think I'm 'wild.'"

"No, the fact is, they were objecting to me back when you were still in diapers."

"Why would they do that?" Harlan wanted to know.

Momma blushed and lowered her eyes. "Because . . . because I didn't have a husband. He run off when Thad was no more than a year old."

"Oh. I'm sorry. I didn't mean to embarrass you."

"It ain't exactly a secret. I reckon there's plenty of folks knows about it. Nobody ever brings it up, but they know."

There was a silence. Thad cleared his throat. "So, I was wondering, if I do go, what should I wear? A feller wouldn't wear overalls to a moving picture, would he?"

"Well, you got them black trousers," Momma said.

"Momma, they come halfway to my knees."

"Why don't I lend you pair, and a shirt, too?" Harlan said. "We're almost the same size."

"You'd do that?"

"I don't see why not. It's not as if you're going to wrestle catfish in them."

Momma smiled at him. "That's kind of you, Mr. James."

"I guess I'm just a natural do-gooder," Harlan said. "Just like cousin Jesse."

Momma's eyes went wide. "You're related to Jesse James?"

"Not really. But around here I seem to be more popular

if I can claim some kind of kinship. It seems that people here consider Jesse something of a hero."

As they cleared the table and washed the dishes, they took turns recounting some of the many dubious tales passed down about Jesse James. Harlan told a story he'd heard about the time old Jesse was given food and lodging by a widow in the vicinity of Neosho. When Jesse asked the woman why she appeared so sad, she revealed that a man from the bank was coming by the next morning to foreclose on her and throw her and her two children out. Jesse asked how much she owed the bank. Two thousand dollars, the widow said. Jesse promptly counted out that amount from his saddlebags and handed it over to the astounded and grateful widow. In the morning Jesse lay in wait alongside the road, and when the bank officer rode by, Jesse relieved him of his money—not all of it, just two thousand dollars.

Thad followed with the legend of Jesse James's gold, which supposedly was buried at Crag O'Lea cave or else at the junction at the Big and Little Sugar, or perhaps over to Lanagan—somewhere in McDonald County, anyway.

Finally Momma got in the spirit of things and consented to tell an incident that had happened to Claib Duval, who was generally agreed to be the oldest man in the county. When Claib was a young reporter for the Pineville paper, he wrote an editorial defending the James boys. One night soon afterward the door to the newspaper office flew open and in strode a tough-looking hombre, wearing a gunbelt and clutching a copy of the paper. He demanded to know who had written that editorial. When Claib owned, a little fearfully, that it was his work, the stranger shook his hand and thanked him, then scrawled something on the paper, tossed it down, and rode off. "When Claib picked up the paper," Momma said, "he saw that the stranger had scribbled his signature on it, and the name he signed was . . ." She paused dramatically, "Harry Bullard!"

Harlan blinked at her in bewilderment. "Who in the world is Harry Bullard?"

Momma smiled slyly. "You know, that's exactly the same thing Claib Duval said."

When Harlan departed around nine o'clock, he left behind the ice chest so the rest of the catfish would keep for a few days. He also left behind a pleasant feeling that was slow to fade.

As Thad walked him to his automobile, Harlan said, "Thanks for inviting me. I had a really enjoyable evening. Your mother is a fine woman, and the catfish wasn't bad, either. I'll bring by a shirt and some pants for you, as promised. Or you can stop by my cabin if you get a chance. You're always welcome." He leaned closer and added, "Particularly if you bring refreshments with you."

"I'll try," Thad told him. "Like I said, I ain't sure he's going to let me have any more after this."

"Tell him that, if he does, I'll buy four or five bottles. I can always take it home to my friends."

After Harlan drove off, Thad slowly mounted the rotting steps to the porch. He stomped on a loose board to put it back in place, and it broke in half. "Durn it, " he said. "This place is falling apart."

But he knew they would never have the money for lumber to repair it properly, no matter how many jars of whiskey he sold. It was lucky they owned the house, such as it was, free and clear, for they could never have come up with money for rent or house payments. That was the one good thing his daddy had ever done, leaving them this house when he ran off.

Momma had changed into her everyday dress and was feeding the beagle pup some leftover catfish. "Your friend Mr. James is a nice man," she said, without looking up.

"He said you were a . . ." Thad was too embarrassed to use Harlan's exact words. "A nice person, too."

She smiled. "Did he?"

"Words to that effect. In case you're wondering, he ain't married."

"I wasn't wondering," she said indignantly. "Well, maybe it crossed my mind. He surely seems to have plenty of cash money! Did he say what he does for a living?"

"He said he's in the tobacco business, that's all."

"He didn't smoke himself, though. That's good. Your daddy, he smoked, and I never did care for it."

"What did he do for a living? I don't believe you ever said."

"He mostly didn't do nothing, just got by on what the government gave him for disability." She stood up. "I was embarrassed, having Mr. James offer to lend you his clothes."

"He don't mind."

"Well, I do. I didn't realize you were so clothes poor. We got to get you a few things to start school in." She took down the lard tin bank and dumped the contents on the table. "It ain't but a few weeks away."

Thad slumped in his chair. "Don't go reminding me."

She looked up from counting the money. "Now, don't you be that way. An education is important, and you know it."

"Momma, what earthly good is a high school diploma going to do me? What job is it going to make me fit for? There ain't no jobs to speak of, and what there are sure don't require no education beyond the ability to write, plus add and subtract some."

"Nobody says you got to stay in Pineville."

"Don't you want me to?"

"I want you to amount to something, that's what I want. I want you to have the things and the oppportunities I never had."

"What about what I want, Momma? I like it here. I got everying I want."

"You want to be dirt poor all your life? You want to live in a house like this one, that's falling down? Because if'n you stay here that's what you'll have, or worse. Don't you want more? Don't you have no ambition?"

Thad shrugged. "I reckon not."

Momma clapped the handful of coins she'd been counting onto the table, and the money flew in all directions. "Then you're no better than your daddy! I reckon it's true what folks say about the apple not falling far from the tree." She rose abruptly from her chair. "I'm going to bed. I got to work breakfast in the morning. Maybe I can take in enough to buy you a shirt that ain't worn out or patched, at least." She pushed past the blanket that covered the bedroom doorway.

Thad got down on his knees and picked up the scattered coins. He scraped the rest of the money carefully into the lard tin, then stood there staring at it and thinking.

As many times as he had stretched the truth in the past—and it had been quite a few—he had always kept a firm hold in his own mind on what was so and what was not. But when he'd said to Momma just then that he had everything he wanted, he'd felt himself to be off balance somehow, as if he'd been sure he was standing with both feet firmly planted on the truth and then it had given way a little under him, like one of those rotten boards on the porch, and suddenly he wasn't so certain where he stood any longer.

Out in the shed, Dauncey started in whining again. Thad could hear his claws scrabbling at the shed door. "Shoot," Thad said. He couldn't leave Dauncey out there all alone.

He slipped quietly into the bedroom and pulled the blanket off his bed, and carried it out to the shed, where he folded it into a makeshift bed. He slept the night there with Dauncey curled up, contented, next to him.

Dayman was a hard one to get to know, and Thad wasn't sure what the man was likely to do or say when he confessed that he'd lost another jar of corn liquor. Thad was tempted to just consider his business relationship with Dayman at an end, but there were several reasons why he couldn't do that.

One was that he owed Dayman for the two jars that

had been stolen or broken, and he couldn't think of any other way of doing that except to work it off by selling more of Dayman's product for him.

Another was that he and Momma needed the extra money pretty badly—assuming he ever started earning money again, instead of going further into the hole. The third reason was that he'd told Harlan James that he could supply him with whisky, and he didn't want to let Harlan down or to go back on his word.

In the morning Thad fed and watered Dauncey and then hurried off so he wouldn't have to hear the hound complain over being locked up and left behind.

Clem Cordell and friends were playing ball on the field across from the school again, and Clem called to him to come and pitch a few, but Thad just waved and went on by.

He took a detour through town, by way of the hardware store, where he caught Willa's eye long enough to signal that he'd got her message and would meet her as arranged.

As he started across the square, he spotted Pearly Rickett sitting in his old Chevrolet, spitting tobacco and watching him. The deputy waved, but Thad put his head down and pretended not to see him. He certainly didn't want Pearly getting the idea that Thad was friendly toward him or even that his momma had told him to act friendly. It might just encourage him to come around more.

Thad was in no hurry to face Dayman, so he took the long route, which was also the easiest to walk. Instead of cutting across country, he hiked up Goodin Hollow Road a couple of miles, then turned and followed the old logging trail that led to the top of what he called Gooseberry Ridge, after the berry bushes that had grown up in some of the logged-off areas.

This year, thanks to the heat and the drought, the bushes were almost bare of fruit. He plucked the few small, dried-up berries there were, and sat on a log to eat them and to catch his breath.

Except for the occasional "squeal, squeal, squeal" of a cardinal or the rustling of a squirrel scampering through the dry leaves, the woods were still. Then he heard a sound that was out of place—the sound of an automobile engine laboring up over the narrow logging road.

Probably just some tourister, Thad thought, hoping to spot one of the razorback hogs that were said to run wild in these hills, or perhaps one of those even more elusive beasts, the gowrow—a meat-eating lizard two feet long, with tusks and a sicklelike tail—and the snawfus, a white deer with supernatural powers.

Since Thad wasn't anywhere near Dayman's still yet, he figured there was no harm in being seen here. But when the automobile chugged into view, it wasn't a tourister's fancy vehicle. It was Pearly Rickett's Chevrolet. And it was too late now for Thad to hide or escape. All he could do was sit there, trying to force a gooseberry down his suddenly constricted throat, while Pearly advanced, his automobile's wheels snapping dead limbs and heaving over rocks.

Thad prayed that the deputy would drive on by, but instead Pearly stopped directly in front of him, shut the engine off, pulled on the handbrake, and climbed out.

"Howdy," Thad said, his voice tight and unnatural sounding.

"Howdy yourself," Pearly said. "What you up to?"

"Not much. Thought I'd pick me some gooseberries, but there ain't much of a crop this year."

Pearly nodded slowly and spit tobacco juice. "I expect you was after something more than just gooseberries. Ain't that so?"

"Well, I had thought about bagging me a red squirrel or two for supper."

Pearly laughed skeptically. "With what? You ain't got no gun, boy."

"Don't need none. I'm a dead shot with a stone."

"Maybe. Anyway, that ain't what I meant, and you know it."

"What did you mean, then?" Thad asked innocently.

"All right, if'n I have to spell it out, I'm a-talking about bootleg whiskey. I know you're a-running it for somebody out here."

"How come you know it, and I don't?"

"I know it because I got evidence. I got the Mason jar you left in that old wreck of a Model T."

Thad tried hard not to let Pearly see the effect the deputy's words had on him. He should have known that was what became of the corn liquor. He'd never worried much about Pearly catching him because he'd always considered the deputy to be pretty much of a fool and not very bright. Apparently he had underestimated the man.

"What makes you think it was me?"

"I don't think it was. I know it was. Bud Durgen seen you stow it there."

"All I stowed there was my brogans."

"Ain't no use trying to lie. I had my eye on you for a long while. Alls I needed was some evidence, and now I got it."

Thad knew there was no point in saying anything more. He just waited to see what Pearly meant to do.

"Now, I could arrest you as an accessory, but I don't want to have to do that. Your momma's a friend of mine, and I don't like to cause her no grief."

"What you mean is you don't want to get her riled at you."

Pearly gave one of his rotten-toothed grins, and Thad looked away. "That, too. But I will tell her if'n I have to. She might even be real grateful to me, for helping to keep her boy from falling in with bad company."

"Even if'n I was selling corn liquor for someone, it ain't as if I was involved with outlaws. They're just trying to make a living."

"Don't matter. The federal government says it's a crime to make your own whiskey, same as robbing a bank or killing somebody, and it's a crime if'n you help sell it, too. That's the law, and it's my job to uphold the law."

"So you're fixing to arrest me?"

"I didn't say that. The way I see it, we might could strike us a bargain."

"A bargain?"

"That's right. You tell me who you're running whiskey for, and where his still is, and I let you off scot-free."

"I can't do that. In the first place, I ain't running whiskey for nobody. In the second place, if'n I was I wouldn't never go and betray him that way. It wouldn't be right."

"You figure it's right to break a federal law?"

"It ain't against ary law I know of to stow your brogans in a broken-down automobile, and that's all I done."

Pearly sighed and rubbed his bulbous nose. "All right, I tell you what. I'll make it so you don't have to tell me right out. I'll do what the Shore Patrol used to do in a situation like this. I'll ask you questions, and you nod if'n I hit it right, okay? That way you won't be betraying nobody. You'll just be a-hinting."

"It still wouldn't be right."

"Well, let's just try her, okay? Now. That feller you been running whiskey for—could it be Coy Rayburn by any chance? What about Elmer Tunney? Frank Gilliam? Dayman Curtiss?"

Thad kept his face expressionless, so as not to give anything away. It was difficult not to react when he mentioned Dayman, for it was the first time he'd ever heard anybody say what Dayman's last name was.

"This ain't a-working, son. I just named all the still operators I know of, and you ain't nodded, even a little bit. Is there some new feller out there I ain't hear about yet?"

Thad didn't reply.

Pearly scowled and launched a stream of tobacco juice that narrowly missed Thad's bare foot. "Your momma said you was stubborn and a liar, and she's right on both counts." He reached for his gunbelt, and for a heart-stopping second Thad thought the deputy was going to draw on him. But all he did was hitch the belt up under his pot belly. "Have it your own way, then. I reckon I'll just have to let your momma know what you've been up to.

And I'll have to keep an even closer eye on you. From here on it don't matter where you go or what you do, you can figure on me being one step behind you."

Pearly stomped over to his vehicle and started it up. When he tried to turn it around, he fetched one fender up against a stump and it caved in with a sickening sound. "Damn!" Pearly shouted, and pounded the steering wheel with the palm of his hand.

Thad knew he shouldn't laugh, but when he saw how red Pearly's face had turned, he couldn't help it. That made Pearly even madder. As he steered the automobile back down the logging road, the deputy pointed a shaking finger in Thad's direction and hollered, "I'm a-going to make you real sorry you didn't cooperate when you had the chance!"

Thad was pretty certain that Pearly's talk about arresting him was so much hot air. So far as he knew, nobody in McDonald County had been put in jail for making whiskey, let alone just selling it. Poly Lane had served time for wounding a revenuer once, but if there was no injury involved the most that ever happened was that revenuers busted up the still, putting its operator out of business for a time, sometimes permanently if he didn't have the money to buy new equipment and supplies.

Thad had no doubt, though, that Pearly meant what he said about watching every move he made, and that could prove to be a problem. No matter how careful he was, it was possible that he might end up leading the law right to Dayman's still.

When it came to the part about telling his momma, Thad wasn't so sure. If Pearly had any hope of getting his momma into a marrying mood, he might not want to jeopardize his chances by accusing her son of a federal crime. On the other hand, as Pearly had said, Momma actually might be grateful to him for letting her know what kind of trouble Thad was in.

The thing he really couldn't figure, though, was why the sheriff's office was suddenly making such a fuss about the selling of a little corn liquor. Neither Pearly nor his brother, the sheriff, had concerned themselves about it before, except when the liquor fell into their laps.

Pearly had mentioned the federal government several times. That made Thad suspect that maybe revenue officers had begun snooping around more seriously than usual, and insisting that local law officers do their part. If that was so, it meant he would have even more eyes watching him, waiting for him to slip up. In fact, there was a good chance that right this minute Pearly or the sheriff or a Federal revenuer had a pair of field glasses trained on him.

The thought made him glance around self-consciously. Though he hated to go back home empty-handed, he couldn't very well go on to Dayman's still now. Nor could he visit Sinking Spring and risk revealing its location. He considered trying to knock down a squirrel, but it didn't make much sense when they still had all that catfish.

12

When he got home Momma was still at the café. Thad knew that Pearly often ate lunch there. He wondered if the deputy was likely to go ahead and spill the beans to Momma, or if he would hold off a while in order to give Thad a chance to reconsider.

The smart thing to do, Thad supposed, would be to steal old Pearly's thunder and tell Momma himself that he'd been running liquor. That way he could tell the story his way, and make it seem as if it wasn't anything much, just something he'd done once or twice, without thinking about the consequences.

On the other hand, what if Pearly was just bluffing? Then Thad would have confessed for no reason. Dauncey's barking interrupted his thoughts. He went out to the shed and, taking the hound by the collar, led him into the house.

To make certain Dauncey didn't wander off, he fastened both screen doors shut with their hook-and-eye fasteners—actually hook-and-bent-nail, for the eyes had long ago worked their way out of the doorjambs.

The beagle pup dashed up to Dauncey, eager to be friends, but Dauncey would have none of it. He tried to act as though the pup did not exist, which wasn't easy. When acting lovable didn't work, the pup resorted to biting Dauncey's ears. Finally the bluetick hound retreated to the bedroom, and wouldn't come out even after Thad fried up some fish for the three of them on the kerosene stove.

They were practically out of kerosene, he noticed. But Momma had worked both breakfast and lunch, so surely they could afford to buy more. She'd also talked about buying school clothing for him, but that could wait.

Thinking about money brought to mind the trip to Anderson that was coming up. How much did it cost to get into a moving picture, anyway? Twenty-five cents, at least, he guessed. Would Willa expect him to pay her way in, too? And what if the girls wanted to go out for ice cream sodas or such as that afterward? He hadn't bought but one ice cream soda all summer, but he recalled that it had set him back fifteen cents, and in Anderson they might even be more. Say they were twenty cents, times two people, that was forty cents, and say fifty cents more for the both of them to get into the moving picture—that was practically a dollar!

Going to the moving pictures promised to be an expensive proposition. He began to wish he had never taken Willa up on her offer. Why had she asked him, anyway? Didn't she know he didn't have money for that sort of thing? Maybe she didn't. Maybe for her a dollar wasn't quite so hard to come by. He was willing to bet that her folks never had to choose between buying school clothing and buying kerosene. In fact, he recalled from the times when he was still allowed to visit Willa, they didn't even cook with kerosene; their stove ran on electricity, the same as their lights.

The front screen door rattled. "Thad?" Momma called. "Are you in there?"

"Coming!" He ran to the door and unfastened the hook from the bent nail. Momma stepped inside, carrying a large paper sack. "I brought Dauncey in for a while," Thad said, "so I thought I'd best keep these doors latched."

"Good. Pearly Rickett says there's been several more reports of rabies."

Thad fastened the door. "Oh. You talked to Pearly, then?"

"I brought him his lunch." She set the sack on the kitchen table. "I waited on Harlan James, too, and he said to give you these." She pulled out a striped shirt and brown pants. "Go ahead and try them on. Let's see how you look."

Thad went into the bedroom and got into Harlan's clothes. The britches were a little long in the legs, but he could roll the cuffs up inside and have Momma pin them. The shirt was starched and pressed, and smelled like a new pencil tablet did on the first day of school.

Thad wished they had a better mirror than the small, cracked one on Momma's dresser, so he could see how he looked. All he had to go by was Momma's reaction. "Well, now, don't you look dashing!"

Thad grinned self-consciously. "I don't know. Do I?"

"Yes, you do. You look like—" She broke off abruptly, floundered for a second, and then finished lamely, "Well, like one of the models in the Sears, Roebuck catalog."

"That ain't what you were about to say, was it?"

"No. I was about to say you looked the way your daddy used to look in his army uniform. But I don't like the thought of you having to wear a uniform someday."

"Well, I got no plans to." He rolled up the sleeves of the shirt part way, as he'd seen Harlan do, and studied how it looked. "I was thinking maybe I ought not to plan on going to that moving picture, neither. It's liable to cost a sight of money."

"Now, you can't not go, not after you promised Minnie. How much do you figure it'll come to?"

"Well, if'n we get us some kind of treat afterwards, it might could be as much as a dollar."

"I reckon we can afford that." She turned the contents of her skirt pocket out on the table. "I took in quite a bit in tips today. Mr. James went and left me ten cents, and all he had was a sandwich and pie." She shook her head as if she disapproved of such profligacy, but she was smiling.

"Sounds to me as if he likes you. How much did Pearly Rickett leave?"

"A nickel, and he had the fifty-cent special."

"Well, I reckon that shows how much store the two of them set by you."

Momma gave him a look of mock exasperation. "I ain't the sort to judge a man by how much money he throws away on me."

"'Course not. But all other things being equal, wouldn't you just as soon have a feller with money as one without?"

"Who says I want any sort of feller at all?"

"You did. You said it would help keep a rein on me. Anyway, it was just one of them—what do you call it?—hypothetical questions." Thad went into the bedroom again to change back into his overalls, and to keep from having to look Momma in the face when he asked, "Did Pearly have anything else to say, besides that about the rabies?"

"He was upset because we run out of pecan pie. That's about it. We were busy, so I didn't have time to chat much. Since when are you interested in what Pearly Rickett has to say, anyhow?"

Thad emerged from the bedroom, buckling his overall straps. Though some folks said he had a real knack for telling a story, he couldn't for the life of him think how to tell this one, or even how to begin.

Then he noticed Momma holding the beagle pup, and a small alarm went off in his head. "Where's Dauncey?" he asked, looking around.

"I thought he was in the bedroom with you."

"No, he ain't!" Thad ran to the front door. The hook that should have been holding it shut was dangling free. Apparently Dauncey had pushed against the bottom of the door hard enough to pull the hook loose from the bent nail. They had been so busy talking and admiring his borrowed clothes that they hadn't even noticed.

Thad burst out onto the porch and nearly broke his ankle when one of the rotted boards caved in under his weight. He recovered and limped into the street, calling, "Dauncey! Here, Dauncey! Come here, boy!" There was no sign of the dog in any direction.

"You see him?" Momma called from the doorway.

"No. Looks like he just run off. I reckon he was tired of being shut up that way."

"You better see if'n you can locate him. I wouldn't like him to run across some coon or possum with rabies, and I know you wouldn't, either."

"Like I said, I don't believe he'd mess with no animal that's acting crazy."

"Go look for him anyway. Just be sure you're back in time to keep your appointment with Miss Minnie Brewer."

Despite what he'd said, Thad couldn't help worrying about his dog. So far as he knew, Dauncey had never encountered a coon or a possum with rabies, so maybe he wouldn't know what to make of it. For that matter, Thad had never seen one, either. He'd heard that they staggered around and foamed at the mouth, but he was pretty sure that that was just when they were far along. Maybe before that happened they went around looking and acting more or less normal, in which case Dauncey would likely do what he always did to coons and possums—chase them.

Thad trotted through the neighborhood, asking everyone if they had seen Dauncey come that way. No one had. Finally Alice Gleason, who was out watering her zinnias in an effort to keep them alive, said she'd seen the hound heading down toward the Big Sugar.

Thad hurried down the hill toward the creek, shouting for Dauncey all the way. Then he walked up Cave Road almost to Crag O'Lea. When the sun got low in the sky, he trudged home again, still calling off and on.

He'd hoped Dauncey might come home for supper, but Momma hadn't seen him return. Thad hated to go off someplace without knowing what had become of his dog, but he allowed that there was nothing more he could do. Dauncey would come home when he was good and ready.

Thad had no appetite for supper. He'd had about all the fish he could stand for a while, anyway. He washed up and got into his borrowed clothes and walked down to Minnie

Brewer's. Every block or so he called for Dauncey. Sometimes he heard a dog barking as if in reply, but it was never the deep, throaty bellow of a bluetick hound.

13

If he and Willa had been going to the moving pictures with anybody but Minnie Brewer and her momma, Thad might have been concerned that word would get back to Willa's folks. But he knew that May Belle Brewer was not likely to give them away.

She and Thad's momma went back a long way. They'd grown up together down near Southwest City. May Belle had been the first to move away, when she married Mr. Brewer, who hailed from Pineville. But when Momma had a falling out with her family—Thad gathered that they'd objected to her marrying his daddy—she'd moved to Pineville, too, partly because May Belle was there.

They didn't see each other much anymore, but Thad knew that Momma still considered May Belle a friend. She was possibly, the only woman in town, in fact, that Momma ever spoke of with anything approaching warmth.

Thad took a roundabout route to the Brewers', not wanting to attract Pearly Rickett's attention. Pearly and Willa's daddy were thick as thieves, and the deputy wouldn't hesitate to tell Mr. Houseman that his daughter was keeping bad company, namely Thad.

Mrs. Brewer answered the door. "Well!" she exclaimed,

looking him up and down. "Ain't you a sight, though!"

Thad grinned, embarrassed. "I didn't rightly know how a feller was expected to dress for the moving pictures."

"You look just fine. Don't he, Willa?"

Willa entered the hallway and gave him a wolf whistle. "I'll say."

"You don't look so bad yourself," Thad said. In fact, she looked as pretty as he'd ever seen her, in a sky blue summer dress, with her sun-streaked brown hair pinned up off her slender neck. "You ought not to whistle that way, though. Ain't you heard that for a girl to whistle brings bad luck?"

"That's pure moonshine," Willa said. "I'll whistle as much as I like." And she launched into an off-key rendition of "Oh, Susanna."

"All right," Thad called over the clamor. "Don't say I didn't warn you."

"And just what do you figure is going to happen?"

"Well, the moving picture could turn out to be terrible."

"With Randolph Scott in it? That ain't likely."

Minnie came up behind her and, to Thad's surprise, slugged her hard on the shoulder. "*Isn't.*"

Willa grimaced but, again to Thad's surprise, didn't hit Minnie in return. "Me and Minnie are trying to improve our speech," she explained, rubbing her arm. "If'n one of us uses bad grammar the other one gets to hit her."

"Ain't ain't exactly bad grammar," Thad pointed out. "Everybody says it."

"Not motion picture stars."

"How do you know? You ever met one?"

"They do interviews all the time in the screen magazines, and not a one of them says ain't." She whirled on Minnie. "That one don't count."

Minnie slugged her anyway, and said smugly, "*Doesn't.*"

The discussion of moving picture stars and their habits continued unabated during the ride to Anderson. So did the grammar lessons. Thad was just as glad that, because of his long legs, he'd been assigned the front seat, out of the way of flying fists.

"Oh, guess what," Willa said. "Mrs. Mitchell told me what she'd picked for the school play. We're going to do *The Importance of Being Earnest* by Oscar Wilde."

"Oh," Thad said.

"I'm trying out, too," Minnie said. "Before you come—*came*—we was—*were*—discussing what our stage names ought to be.

"Stage names?" Thad echoed.

"Of course," Willa said. "Actors and actresses practically never use their real names, you know. You think Anne Sheridan's real name is Anne?"

"I never thought about it."

"Well, it ai—isn't!" Minnie's fist stopped in midair, and Willa went on. "It's Clara. And Robert Taylor's name is Spangler Brugh, for heaven's sake. Randolph Scott's real name is George."

Minnie struck a fake glamorous pose. "I've decided my stage name is going to be Lila Lamont."

"And I'm going to change mine to Virginia Lee."

"Sounds like some old Confederate general," Thad observed. "I don't see what's wrong with your real name."

"Willa? It sounds like a tree. And with the Houseman, I sound like a tree house."

Minnie giggled. "It does sound like that, don't it? Ow!" It seemed to Thad that Willa hit her harder than was necessary.

"Settle down, girls," said Mrs. Brewer mildly. "It ain't ladylike to have bruises on your shoulders."

"You get a hit, Momma," Minnie squealed. "You said ain't."

"You hit me and I'll say it again, and this time it'll be about the moving picture, as in 'You ain't going.'"

Willa leaned up closer to Thad. "We got to pick out a good name for you now."

Thad made a face. "The one my momma and daddy give me suits me fine."

"I expect it was purely your Momma's doing," Mrs. Brewer said.

"Why do you say that?"

"Well, because your daddy had—" Mrs. Brewer broke off. "Maybe your momma would prefer me not to talk about it."

"No, it's all right," Thad lied. "She told me all about him, and about how he run off before I was ever born." The truth was, he'd had not notion that his daddy had abandoned them that early on. How could he just up and leave, Thad wondered, knowing he had a child on the way?

"Ran," Minnie said, and reached over the seat to punch him on the arm.

"What?" Thad said, startled.

"You said he run off. It should be ran."

"All right, girls," Mrs. Brewer said, more sternly this time. "That's about enough of that." She gave Thad an apologetic glance. "They ain't usually quite this wound up. It must be having a good-looking, well-dressed feller along that does it."

"Momma!" Minnie wailed.

Though it wasn't nearly dark when they arrived, the moving picture theater was all lit up. A sign above the entrance read "Randolph Scott, Barbara Stanwyck in *Outlaw Trail*." Around the border of the sign alone were more electric light bulbs than were strung around the dance pavilion at Shadow Lake on a Saturday night.

A dozen people were lined up before a little booth on the front of the building. On the booth was a smaller sign that read "Admission. Adults 30¢. Children 12 and under 15¢." Thad winced and fingered the coins in his pocket. Thirty cents was even more than he'd bargained for. As if reading his mind, Willa leaned over and said softly, "I brought my own money. I got enough to pay for you, too. It's only fair, since I invited you."

"Thanks, but I'm okay."

"If'n you're sure. Where'd you get the nice shirt and britches?"

"They belonged to my daddy. Momma says he always dressed nice."

Since he'd got by so cheaply on the tickets, Thad insisted on paying for the popcorn. He got himself the large size; the lack of supper was beginning to catch up with him.

Though Thad had nothing to compare it with, the moving picture seemed good enough. Even so, he had trouble keeping his mind on it. He kept wondering about Dauncey, whether or not the dog got home safely, and about Pearly Rickett, whether or not he would tell Momma that Thad was running whiskey.

Sitting there in Harlan's clothes made him think about Harlan, too, and those thoughts got mixed up with his thoughts about his daddy, so that when he tried to picture what his daddy might have looked like, as he had done so often in the past, he found himself picturing someone who looked a lot like Harlan James.

He forced himself to concentrate on the picture, knowing that Willa would want to talk about it afterward. He'd assumed that Randolph Scott would be the good guy, but instead he was a member of an outlaw gang that robbed banks and held up trains.

As outlaws went, he wasn't bad. He used good grammar and he made it a point never to shoot anybody while committing these robberies. He even had a fist fight with one of the really bad outlaws, and broke the fellow's jaw.

Actually the sheriff, who a body would think was the good guy, was far less appealing than Randolph Scott. He didn't shave regularly, he had terrible manners, and he kept trying to talk Randolph Scott's girl, Barbara Stanwyck, into marrying him.

Thad was surprised and gratified when it turned out that Randolph Scott was really a Pinkerton detective who was just pretending to be an outlaw in order to get the goods on the real outlaws. During the final shoot-out, Thad counted the number of times Randolph Scott fired his gun without visibly reloading: fourteen—a lot less than Clem Cordell had indicated.

The actual bad guy did not throw his empty gun at Randolph Scott, either. He didn't have a chance to, because he got his foot caught in his stirrup and was dragged to death.

"How did you like it?" Willa asked as they left the theater.

"Pretty good. I liked all the gunfights. I got to get me a gun."

Willa shook her head. "Men. What about the love story? Didn't you—"

"Willa!" Minnie poked her urgently.

"What?" Willa protested. "I didn't say nothing wrong!"

"No, it ain't that! Look over there!" She made small, frantic pointing motions close to her chest.

Willa peered around Thad and gasped. "Oh, no!"

"What?" Thad asked. And then he saw her—Mrs. Hilyard, the worst gossip in Pineville, a town full of gossips. She was standing at the edge of the throng of departing moviegoers, glaring straight at them.

"She seen us!" Willa said. "She'll tell my folks, I know she will!"

"Maybe not," Thad said. But he knew Willa was right. The woman was constitutionally unable to keep anything to herself. "Durn it. I told you, didn't I?"

"Told me what?"

"About how bad luck is brought on by whistling. It never fails."

14

On the way home, Willa failed to discuss the Randolph Scott Western in the usual detail. In fact, she didn't say much at all. Thad was pretty sure she was rehearsing what she would say to her folks, and anticipating what they would say to her.

"I could tell them it was my idea," Thad offered. "They already have a bad opinion of me. It won't hurt none to add to it."

"No," Willa said. "They know you ain't the sort to propose going to no motion picture."

Minnie let this glaring lapse in grammar slip by. Thad suspected she had drifted off to sleep in the dark backseat. Willa fell silent again.

"That refrigerated air in that theater was downright cold, wasn't it? Mrs. Brewer said.

"I'll say," Thad agreed. "I almost wished I'd brought me a jacket along." Of course, he didn't have but one, and it was no great shakes. It would have looked awfully shabby over top of his daddy's good shirt and—Thad shook his head. He must be getting drowsy, too. For a second he'd actually let himself believe that these fine clothes had belonged to his daddy.

He glanced back at Willa. She appeared to be asleep now. Thad turned to Mrs. Brewer and said quietly, "I guess you knew my daddy, then?"

"Oh, yes. I didn't know him very well, but I knew his family. Everybody in Southwest City knew the Curtisses."

103

"Curtisses?" Thad echoed, puzzled. "Ain't his name the same as mine?"

Mrs. Brewer gave him a startled glance. "Why, no. McCune was your momma's name."

As soon as she said it, Thad realized that of course that was so. He'd just never thought about it. He'd had no occasion to. He hadn't met his momma's family but once or twice, and that was when he was a young boy. Whenever she spoke about them, which was seldom, she just called them Momma or Your Aunt Lorena or Your Cousin Ed, with no last name attached. He didn't recall ever hearing her say his daddy's last name, or making any mention at all of his family.

"Well, didn't she take his name, though, after they were married?" Thad asked, still confused.

Mrs. Brewer stared at him a moment, before saying softly, "They never did marry, Thad. I thought you knew that. That's why your momma's folks mostly won't have nothing to do with her. That, and the fact that your daddy come from the sort of family he did."

"Why? What were they like?"

"It ain't my place to say. You best ask your momma about it."

"I have. She don't ever want to talk about it. I figure I got a right to know. Can't you tell me anything? I won't let on to momma."

Mrs. Brewer sighed. "Well, just let me say that they weren't what you'd call model citizens. J. D.'s daddy was a drunk, and a mean one. His sister was—well, she was free with her affections and his brothers were, by all accounts, horse thieves at the very least. J. D. was far the best of the bunch, but I'm afraid that ain't saying much."

"J. D.?"

"That's what most folks called your daddy. Your momma insisted on calling him John. She thought it sounded more refined. For a time it looked as if your momma might make something out of him. But then J. D. went off to the war, before he even finished school, and when he come back he was like a different person, all bitter and strange. Your momma thought she could nurse him back to his old self, I guess. You know how she is about taking in things that are sick and wounded."

"I know. Do you have any notion of where he might be now?"

Mrs. Brewer abruptly sat up in her seat, as though she'd begun to drift off, too. "I told you more than I ought to of already. Like I said, it ain't my place. If'n your momma wanted you to know these things, she'd of told you by now."

"I expect she's been waiting until she felt I was old enough to handle it. Sometimes she don't realize I'm thirteen. She still thinks of me as a young boy."

"I know just how she feels. We mommas all have a tendency to want to protect our children from the harsh truth."

Though Thad resented the way Momma had withheld the facts about his daddy all these years, he was in no position to blame her for it. It would be a case of the pot calling the kettle black, for sure. After all, how many times had he hidden the truth from her, or made up his own version of it, and justified it by saying that if he told her the actual truth, it would only make her worry more?

When Mrs. Brewer dropped him off at his house, he opened the door of the automobile quietly, not wanting to wake the girls. "Tell Willa I'm real sorry. I hope her folks ain't too hard on her. And thanks for what you told me."

"You're not to let on to your momma, remember?"

"I won't." He slid out and softly pushed the door shut.

Momma had left a light burning in the kitchen for him. He went around to the back door. As he passed the shed, there was an explosion of whining and scratching from inside. "Dauncey!" Thad yanked the shed door open and slipped in. He couldn't see Dauncey in the dark, but the way the hound squirmed and licked his face, there was no mistaking who it was. "You old rapscallion!" he scolded. "Where'd you get off to?"

He ran his hand over Dauncey's body, feeling for any sort of cut or scrape that might indicate that he'd tangled with a wild animal. He found nothing worse than a few dock burrs and some Spanish needles that pricked his fingers.

"You surely gave me a fright. No more running off like that, you hear? From now until cold weather, the only way you can go out is if you're tied to a piece of rope, okay?"

Dauncey barked as if in agreement to these terms. Thad checked to make sure the dog had food and water, then rumpled Dauncey's ears one last time. "Settle yourself down, now. I'll see you in the morning."

As Thad undressed for bed, he heard his momma stirring on the other side of the sheet they'd hung to divide the bedroom in two. "How was your date with Minnie?"

"Fine. The moving picture wasn't too realistic, but it

was exciting." He was going to leave it at that, but for some reason he added, "Willa Houseman decided to come along, too."

"That's nice," she murmured. Thad suspected she was more than half asleep. Otherwise she'd have said something more like, "Her folks let her go with you?" Still, he'd done his part. He'd told her the truth. If she didn't necessarily take it in, that wasn't his fault.

In the morning Thad carefully folded the shirt and britches Harlan James had loaned him and put them in the paper sack. "Everybody said how good these looked," he told Momma. "Wish I could afford some like them or even half as decent."

Momma gave him a perplexed look. "I never knew you to be concerned about clothes before."

"I ain't concerned, exactly. It was just kind of nice, getting bragged on that way. I guess Harlan must be used to it. He's got all kinds of expensive things—an automobile, fishing gear. I bet he has him some fancy guns, too. Maybe not as good as Randolph Scott's. I don't believe they make one that will shoot fourteen times." He paused, then added, "I'll bet my daddy had him a gun when he was my age, didn't he?"

"Most likely. I don't recall."

"I reckon it was just the war that soured him on them, was it?"

Momma sighed. "Thad. Go and give Mr. James back his clothes. I should of washed them first, but I could never starch and press them that nice. He must take them to a laundry."

When Thad got to the Elk River Resort, Harlan James' Dodge was gone. Thad couldn't help feeling a little relieved. He hadn't been looking forward to telling Harlan that he couldn't sell him the corn liquor as promised, not until Pearly Rickett got off his back, anyway, and by then Harlan would probably have headed home.

He left the clothing on the little front porch of Harlan's cabin and walked uptown, just in time to encounter Clem Cordell coming out of the drugstore with what looked suspiciously like a poke full of candy.

"How'd you like that Western picture?" Clem asked.

"Pretty good. It had a lot of shooting, and not much reloading."

"I told you, didn't I? How's your arm?"

"It's okay. Why?"

"Thought I might still be able to talk you into pitching for the Panthers. The playoffs are next week, and Lanagan's got a real ball of fire on the mound."

"I'd listen better if'n I had a couple of those chocolates."

"They ain't chocolates. If'n they was, they'd be melted chocolates, in this heat."

"What are they, then?"

"Licorice."

"That'll do."

Clem grudgingly held out the poke. Thad fished out a licorice whip and chewed on it. "Now will you pitch for us?" Clem asked.

"Not for one licorice whip."

"How about the whole bag?"

"Sorry. Like I said, it's too much like work."

"How about that twenty-two I told you about, then? I'll let you have it for three dollars and a promise to pitch for the Panthers. That's practically giving it away, boy."

"You know, I just might take you up on that—if'n I had three dollars, which I don't."

Clem scowled. "All right, you can owe it to me, then."

"I can't do that. I can't go into debt, not knowing if I'll ever be able to pay it back. I owe a feller eight dollars already."

"What for?"

"It's a long story. Listen, could I get you to do something for me?"

"Why should I? You won't do nothing for me."

"This is something real easy." Thad reached out and tore a square of paper from Clem's candy poke.

"Hey!" Clem protested.

Thad pulled a pencil stub from his bib pocket and painstakingly printed on the paper *Meet me out back.* "Give this to Willa Houseman, could you? And don't let her folks see you doing it."

Thad waited by the backhouse behind Houseman's Hardware. Within five minutes Willa emerged from the rear and hurried over to him. She didn't greet him with her usual smile.

"From the look on your face, I'd say your folks found out."

Willa nodded. "Father was furious. He called you a lot of things I won't repeat, and told me I wasn't much better. They said I ain't to go to no more moving pictures for two months, and worst of all, they"—Her voice broke.—"they said I ain't to try out for the school play."

"What? Why not?"

"They said if'n they couldn't trust me, then I'd have to come straight home after school." Her voice faltered again, and she dashed away a tear that was poised to slide down her cheek. "It ain't fair. They know how much that play means to me."

"I could tell them it was my idea, going to the moving picture," Thad said, not very enthusiastically, "that I talked you into it."

Willa shrugged. "Might as well not bother. They won't listen anyhow." She took a deep breath. "Well, this will blow over, I reckon. In the meanwhile, they can't stop us from seeing one another at school. I got to go in now. I told them I had to go to the backhouse. I can't take but so much time for that." She gave a little laugh that threatened to turn into something else, then whirled and ran inside.

Thad headed down toward the Big Sugar, wondering what do to with himself. His options seemed to have suddenly become awfully limited. He couldn't go exploring with Dauncey unless he kept the dog on a rope. He couldn't spend time with Willa. He couldn't deliver Dayman's product for him, or even go to Sinking Spring without wondering whether Pearly Rickett or some revenuer was on his tail.

He cut a hickory sapling and tied some line to it and tried his luck at fishing. He caught a couple of sunfish, but he let them go. Now that he'd experienced the excitement of landing a fifty-pound catfish, the sunfish just didn't seem worth bothering with.

His makeshift fishing gear seemed pitiful and paltry to

him, too, compared with the rod and reel Harlan had let him use. Thad untied the line and jammed it back into his bib pocket. He was about to fling the hickory stick away, but then he thought better of it. Instead he leaned it up against the trunk of a sycamore tree on the bank. Some young boy who didn't know any better might happen by and be glad to have himself a ready-cut fishing pole, crude though it was.

15

Without any particular purpose in mind Thad followed the Big Sugar downstream and found himself at Elk River Resort again. This time the Dodge convertible was parked next to Harlan's cabin, and Harlan was scrubbing it with a rag and a bucket of water. When he spotted Thad, he grinned and waved.

"These back roads around here are two inches deep in dust. Well, only one inch deep, now, because the other inch is on my car."

"You got another rag? I'll help."

"I appreciate it." Harlan tossed him a towel off the front seat. It was a little frayed and stained, but every bit as good as the bath towels that Thad and Momma used for drying themselves.

"You sure you want me to use this?"

"Sure. It's no good."

Thad shrugged and dipped it in the soapy water. "You been out fishing?"

"No. Just scouting for likely tobacco-growing land."

"Find anything?"

"A couple of possibilities."

"I guess you got the poke with your shirt and britches. I'm obliged for the loan of them. Momma says she's sorry for not washing and ironing them, but she was afraid she wouldn't get it right."

"That's fine. I'm sure she has enough to do already. How was the movie?"

"Well, aside from the fact that me and Willa was seen together, it was pretty good."

Harlan gave him a surprised look. "Somebody objects to the two of you keeping company?"

"Her folks do. They don't consider me good enough for her."

"Because you peddle a little whiskey?"

"No, they ain't even aware of that, so far as I know. It's because we're poor, I guess, or because I'm a woods colt, or both."

Harlan laughed. "A woods colt?"

"That's just a polite name for a body who don't know who his daddy is."

"And you don't?"

"I know his name was J. D. Curtiss, and that he was in the War, and that he didn't like guns, and that's about it." After he said that, Thad remembered what he'd told Harlan about his daddy being the sheriff and getting killed by bank robbers. Harlan had apparently forgotten, for he didn't bring it up. Or maybe he'd seen through the story when Thad had told it.

"The way you say that, I'm guessing you do like guns."

"I don't exactly know. I never had much chance to try one. I'd like to, though."

Harlan's smile hinted that, unlike Momma, he understood all about boys and guns. "Well, let's finish up here, and then we'll see what we can do about that."

Thad's mood went abruptly from glum to excited. "You mean it?"

"Only if you do a good job of car washing," Harlan said. A moment later he added, "Whoa, now! You only need to scrub the dirt off, not the paint!"

As Thad was shining the windshield, Harlan reached under the front seat and came up with a fine-looking twenty-two rifle and a box of shells. "Where do people go around here to do a little target shooting?"

"The dump, I reckon."

"Good enough," said Harlan. "Climb in."

As they headed out Noel road, Thad said, "You never told me you was a hunter."

"I'm not, really. I carry this for protection."

"There ain't nothing very dangerous in these parts, now that the wolves and bears are mostly wiped out."

"What about the gowrows?"

"They keep to themselves."

"It's not the animals I'm concerned about, anyway. It's the people."

Thad laughed. "Shoot. You been listening to too many stories about ornery hillbillies. Nobody around here is likely to give you no trouble—unless you happen to come upon a feller's whiskey still when he ain't expecting you."

"Well, that's possible. I've been on some pretty deserted stretches of road."

"No still I ever heard of was within shouting distance of ary road."

"Then I don't suppose I have to worry about coming across one accidentally. How in the world do they get all that equipment so far back in the woods?"

"One piece at a time, I reckon."

Harlan shook his head. "That sounds like a lot of work for so little profit."

"So little? Five dollars a jar seems like a lot to me."

"Well, that depends on how many jars you sell. Speaking of which, are you planning on paying a visit to your supplier soon? I have no objection to iced tea and cream soda, but a man can stand only so much of it."

Thad's mood swung back over toward glum again. "I wish I could oblige you, Harlan, but I can't. The sheriff's deputy found out I been running whiskey. He's the one took that jar I was fixing to give you. Now he says he's keeping an eye on every move I make. I expect he's hoping I'll lead him to Daym—to my supplier."

Harlan nodded sympathetically. "That's too bad. I imagine you could use the money."

"That ain't no lie. I was hoping to buy me a gun from this friend of mine, so I could hunt game for Momma and me, instead of depending on rocks."

"Rocks?" Harlan said incredulously.

Thad shrugged. "I've got pretty good at knocking down squirrels and rabbits that way. A gun would be a lot more reliable."

"Maybe. But they can be dangerous, too, if you don't know how to handle them properly."

The dump wasn't an official one, just a sinkhole alongside the road where folks brought what trash they couldn't burn. Harlan pulled off the road next to a mostly bald horsehair sofa that someone had been too lazy to drag a few extra yards. "Why don't we carry this over there," Harlan said. "It'll make a good stand for our targets."

"Targets?" Thad said as they walked the sofa to the edge of the sinkhole.

Harlan picked up several glass bottles and lined them up on the back of the sofa. "Targets."

Shooting a gun wasn't as simple a task as it seemed. Harlan showed him just how to hold the twenty-two, how to sight down the barrel with one eye closed, how to hold his breath, how to squeeze the trigger slowly. Thad followed his instruction exactly, except for one thing: each time he knew the gun was about to go off, his right eye closed in anticipation, and it spoiled his aim.

After half an hour and a couple dozen bullets, only one of the row of bottles had bit the dust. "They didn't have this kind of trouble in that Western picture," Thad complained. "They just pointed the gun in the general direction and let it rip."

"Well," said Harlan, "that's the problem with movies. They give you false expectations. They make you think that the way things happen up there on the screen is the way they're supposed to happen in real life as well. But in real life you have to keep your eye open in order to see the target. Try it again, now."

Thad held his right eye open so hard it hurt, and still he blinked it shut at the instant the gun went off. The shot sent a tin can flying off to one side of the sofa, but the bottles remained unscathed. "I can't do it!" he protested.

"That's what you said about landing that catfish, too. And do you remember what I told you?"

"If you say you can't, then you never will, or words to that effect." Thad sighed. "All right. I *can* do it, then." He pulled back the bolt, releasing the spent shell, and inserted a new round. "I can do it." When he tried to push the bolt forward, it wouldn't go. "What's wrong with it?" he demanded.

"Relax. You've got the shell jammed, that's all." Harlan took the twenty-two and examined it. "The ammunition is the problem, I think. I should have brought some with me, instead of buying it locally. These shells are so old they have steel casings instead of brass, and they're a little rusty." He worked the cartridge loose, inserted a new one, and handed the gun back to Thad. "There. You'll just have to work through the shells and find the best ones."

Thad sighted on a brown beer bottle atop the sofa, murmuring over and over to himself, "I can do this. I can do this." He gritted his teeth and slowly, slowly squeezed the trigger. "I can do this." The gun jumped against his shoulder, but this time he didn't flinch. The beer bottle exploded. "I'll be durned," Thad breathed. "I done it."

On the way home, Harlan was silent, as if mulling something over. After a while he said, "I take it your mother has a hard time putting food on the table sometimes."

Thad's pride wouldn't let him admit just how hard.

"We do all right. I just wish I could contribute more."

"And you could if you had a gun?"

"I could try."

Harlan nodded, then turned thoughtful again for a time before he went on. "I suppose you'll have access to some sort of weapon sooner or later, anyway. It may as well be a good one."

Thad blinked at him, puzzled. "Beg pardon?"

"I was just thinking that you might hang on to that one for a few days and see what kind of hunter you are."

Thad was struck speechless. Finally he said, "Your gun? You mean it?"

"Have I ever said anything I didn't mean?"

"I reckon not. You'd truly trust me with it?"

"I trusted you with my rod and reel, didn't I? Who knows what you might bring home this time. A mountain lion, maybe, or a gowrow."

Thad laughed. "Now don't be giving me none of them false expectations."

"I just want you to promise me that you'll handle it responsibly. No loading it until you get out in the woods. And no pointing it at another person, not even in fun."

"I wouldn't do that."

"I didn't imagine you would. It's just that when boys see guns being treated so carelessly in movies, sometimes it gives them ideas. Oh, and while you're out there hunting, why don't you see if you can hunt up a jar of that corn liquor for me?"

"It's like I said, I can't—"

"Ah-ah!" Harlan held up a hand. "What did I tell you about that word? You just let me know when you'll be going, and I'll see to it that Deputy Sheriff Rickett is otherwise occupied. Deal?"

Thad grinned and took Harlan's hand. "Deal."

16

Thad set out right after breakfast the next morning, while it was still halfway cool. When Dauncey heard him leaving, the hound whined so pitifully that Thad didn't have the heart to leave him behind.

He hunted up a ten-foot length of rope and tied one end securely to Dauncey's collar. Though Dauncey was used to roaming around at will, he seemed content for now to stay within the range of the rope.

Thad laid the empty twenty-two in the crook of one arm, the way Harlan had showed him. Half a box of cartridges weighed down one pocket of his overalls, and an old sugar sack hung from a strap around his neck, for use as a game bag.

Harlan's plan to distract Pearly Rickett was a simple one: he would offer to buy the deputy breakfast at the café. Thad was pretty certain that Pearly would never think of turning down a free meal. Momma was waiting tables there this morning. Thad laughed aloud, imagining what a pair Harlan and Pearly would make. It would be very instructive for Momma to see them side by side that way. It would make Pearly appear even less appealing than he did alone, and would at the same time point up how well dressed and well mannered Harlan was.

It couldn't help but make Momma aware of how little she'd be settling for if she settled for the likes of Pearly Rickett.

Thad headed in the general direction of Dayman's hollow. He didn't know whether or not Dayman was likely to entrust him with any more corn liquor, but in any case he owed Dayman an explanation as to why he hadn't come around with the money for the last batch.

As he neared the top of the first ridge, a flock of quail burst from the tall grass, their wings whirring. Dauncey barked and ran to the end of the rope, but Thad held on to him tightly. He didn't bother to load the rifle. He wasn't ready to try a moving target, particularly not one as small as a quail.

When they left the clearing and entered the woods, a red squirrel scampered across their path. Dauncey yanked on the rope so hard that it nearly pulled Thad off his feet. Thad felt badly for the hound who, for reasons that he surely couldn't comprehend, was being kept from doing what he loved best. What would it really hurt if he let Dauncey run loose? The dog never wandered off very far. Anyway, the chances of his running across a rabid animal were pretty slim. And even if he did, Thad could easily bring the animal down now that he had a rifle.

"Here, boy," Thad said. Dauncey came to him whining in frustration, and Thad untied the rope. "You stick around where I can see you, now, you hear?"

Dauncey gave a satisfied bark and turned to go after the squirrel that had dared to challenge him. It was clinging upside down to a post oak, scolding them. Thad slid one of the shells carefully into the chamber of the twenty-two, then knelt on the ground and propped his left arm on his knee to steady it.

Even without repeating "I can do it," he managed to keep his right eye open. An instant after the gun went off, the squirrel tumbled to the ground. Thad shook his head slightly, a bit surprised by how easy it had been—almost too easy. Dauncey picked the carcass up gently in his jaws and carried it to Thad, who noted that the shot had broken the squirrel's back, then slipped it into the sugar sack game bag.

In the hollow behind them was a tiny, unnamed creek that flowed into the Little Sugar. This time of year there wasn't enough water in it to actually flow, just enough to form small, isolated pools. Dauncey trotted eagerly down the hillside to the creek. "You wait up, now!" Thad called. The dog slowed down, but still he got to the bottom of the hollow well before Thad, and began lapping at the water in one of the pools.

Thad was a couple of dozen yards off when he saw something burst through the thick growth of little willow saplings along the creek and launch itself at Dauncey. It was a second or two before he recognized the shape as that of a raccoon. Startled, Dauncey flung himself to one side; his paws slipped on the wet rocks and he plunged into the pool. He came up spraying water and looking astonished at being attacked by an animal that, always before, had been inclined to run from him.

Thad was taken aback, too. Ordinarily a coon would fight only if it were cornered, and this one hadn't been. The only other thing that would account for that kind of aggressiveness was if the coon had babies nearby, and it was late in the year for that.

Or, he realized suddenly, if it was crazy from rabies. "Dauncey!" he shouted. "Come here, boy!"

But though the hound was not one to pick a fight, neither was he one to back down when a fight was forced upon him. The coon had taken up a position on the near bank and was snarling and swiping at the dog with its claws—claws that Thad had seen open up the arm of an unwary coon hunter to the bone. He'd mistaken a stunned animal for a dead one.

"God durn it, Dauncey!" Thad hollered, so fiercely that his voice broke. "Get away from there!" But Dauncey had moved in on his attacker and was dodging its claws, looking for an opening. With shaking hands, Thad fumbled in his pocket for a twenty-two shell. He came up with one, pulled back the rifle bolt, and thrust the shell into the chamber. But when he tried to push the bolt forward, it jammed.

Frantically he rattled the bolt and pounded on the stock, trying to dislodge the rusty shell. He raised his eyes for a moment and saw the coon rake its claws across Dauncey's chest. The hound staggered back and sat down on his haunches in the water. "No!" Thad yelled. He let the rifle drop and plunged down the hill, hoping to chase the coon off. But the animal seemed not even to be aware of him, only of the dog, who was gamely trying to defend himself even though it was clear that whatever fight he had left was draining from him fast, along with the blood that seeped from the gash on his chest, turning the muddy water in the pool pink.

Thad knew that nothing short of laying a stick up alongside its head would discourage the coon: He knew, too, that by the time he could find himself a stick and get to the creek bank, it would be too late. The animal would already have sunk its small, sharp teeth into Dauncey's throat.

He pause, snatched up an egg-sized chunk of chert and, in almost the same motion, let it fly. The stone caught the coon in the ribs. It let out an almost human shriek and whirled around to face its new adversary, baring its teeth and gums, which were flecked with foam. Thad was ready with a second stone. He flung it with all his strength. This time his aim was better. It struck the coon squarely on one ear. The animal crumpled abruptly and lay still.

Though he was gasping for breath, Thad ran on to the creek, scooped up Dauncey in his arms, and laid the dog on the grass. Dauncey mustered enough strength to lift his head and lick Thad's face. "Aw, Dauncey!" Thad cried brokenly, forcing back the sobs that rose in his throat. "I told you not to get so far away, didn't I? Now look at you!"

The only cloth he had to bandage the wound with was his bandanna. He wadded it up and bound it in place with a piece of fishing line. Then he bent and hoisted Dauncey onto his shoulders. Now that Thad wasn't driven by panic, the dog seemed far heavier to him. He had a hard time staying upright with the weight pressing on the back of his neck. But he couldn't leave Dauncey up here and fetch help; the dog would surely bleed to death in the meantime.

He took several deep breaths, then stumbled over the hill, pausing to pick up the twenty-two and stuff the stock of it into the sugar sack alongside the dead squirrel. The barrel banged against his ribs as he plodded on. Sweat mixed with Dauncey's blood trickled down his back.

His legs nearly gave out before he reached to top of the ridge. He leaned against a blackjack oak for a moment, his chest heaving, his shoulder muscles throbbing. "Don't worry, boy," he said, hoarsely. "We'll make it."

It was less of a strain going downhill, but he was so exhausted now that it was all he could do to keep from pitching forward and rolling headlong down into the Little Sugar. Somehow, though, he kept on until he reached the highway. He turned and followed the road, meaning to cross the Elk River on the bridge. But before he made it that far he saw a familiar green convertible heading toward him.

"What happened?" Harlan called.

Thad could barely get the words out. "Coon. Tore him all up. Got to get him home."

Harlan swung the passenger door open. Thad collapsed on the seat and let Dauncey's weight slide into his lap. The dog barely stirred. "Isn't there a veterinarian in town?" Harlan asked.

Thad shook his head. "Anderson."

"Then that's where we'll take him. Hang on." Harlan made a tire-squealing turnaround and headed back up the river, going sixty.

When Thad got his wind back, he said, "I can't afford no veterinarian, Harlan."

"You can't let your dog die, either. I'll take care of it."

"I'm obliged. I'll pay you back as soon as I can."

"We'll see," Harlan said, sounding as though he wasn't counting on it.

17

By the time they got him to Anderson, Dauncey had lost a lot of blood. Still, the vet seemed confident that he'd pull through. When he was done sewing up the dog's wound, he came out onto the porch where Harlan and Thad were waiting. "Did you kill the coon?"

"Yes sir. I brained it with a rock."

Harlan looked at him in surprise. "Why didn't you shoot it?"

Thad scowled. "I got hold of one of them bad shells, and it jammed."

"Too bad you didn't bring along the carcass," the vet said. "I could have tested it for rabies."

"Can't you tell if'n Dauncey's got it or not?"

"Not until the symptoms show up. Rabies gets passed on through the saliva of the infected animal, and there are wounds on your dog's paw that looked as though they could be from a bite. But then again, they might not be."

"They were fighting practically in the creek," Thad said. "I always heard that an animal that had rabies wouldn't go nowhere near water."

"Sorry, but I'm afraid that's just a bit of moonshine."

"If it does prove to be rabies," Harlan said, "isn't there a vaccine you can give him?"

The vet shook his head regretfully. "If the symptoms turn up, all we can do is put him down."

"You mean kill him?" Thad cried.

"It'll be painless—a shot that puts him to sleep. You'd

best leave him, so I can keep an eye on him. We'll know one way or the other in ten to fifteen days."

As they drove home, Thad said, "You reckon he'll be all right?"

"Sure," Harlan said. "He'll be fine."

They rode in silence for a time. Finally, Thad said, "I should of listened to Momma. I should of left Dauncey in the shed."

"Yes," Harlan said. "You should have."

"I just couldn't bear to hear him carrying on so. He didn't have no notion why he was being locked up. It didn't seem fair."

"Things often aren't. But sometimes you have to do a thing that doesn't seem fair on the face of it, in order to head off something else that's a lot worse. I hope you'll remember that."

"I'll try." Thad had the feeling that maybe Harlan was referring to something else, beyond and besides just what had happened to Dauncey, but he couldn't make out what it might be.

"Thanks for bringing the rifle back," Harlan said. "I know you had other things to worry about."

"I couldn't just leave it." Thad peered into the sugar sack, which he'd left on the floor of the automobile. "I brought back a red squirrel, too."

"Did you use a rock or a rifle?"

Thad grinned faintly. "A rifle." He let out a weary sigh. "I don't know what I'd of done if'n you hadn't happened by." He glanced over at Harlan. "How come you to be out there, anyway? I thought you was supposed to be having breakfast with Pearly Rickett."

"I couldn't locate him. I wanted to make sure he wasn't on your tail after all."

"Not that I noticed. I wasn't able to get no whiskey, you know."

Harlan shrugged. "It doesn't matter. I'm not sure I'd be here long enough to drink it anyway."

Thad stared at him. "What do you mean? You ain't leaving right away?"

"Soon. I'm not having any luck finding anything. Everyone thinks I'm a rich tourist, so they're asking double what the land is worth."

"Maybe you ain't going about it the right way. Maybe you got to be more underhanded, like Mr. Houseman. He buys folks' land out from under them when they can't pay the taxes on it."

"That's not exactly underhanded. It's perfectly legal."

"Maybe," Thad said. "But I reckon being legal ain't always the same as being right, any more than illegal is the same as wrong."

Harlan gave him a skeptical look. "That's the sort of philosophy that would have appealed to Jesse James."

"I ain't saying its right to rob banks and shoot folks."

"I'm glad to hear that. I'd hate to think I put a rifle in the hands of a desperate outlaw." Harlan pulled up in front of Thad's house. "You're welcome to hang on to that gun for another day or two and do some more hunting."

"If'n you don't care. Maybe I can find some better ammunition for it." Thad got out with the rifle in his arms. "I got to say, I wish you didn't have to leave, and not just because of the rifle."

To his surprise, Harlan responded with an odd sort of laugh, devoid of any humor. "You'll get over it," he said. Then he put the automobile in gear and drove away.

Telling Momma about what happened to Dauncey was like digging out a festering black locust thorn—it hurt to have to do it, but it felt considerably better once he had. Though Momma was obviously disappointed that he'd been so irresponsible, she didn't scold him or say how she hoped he was sorry, or even ask how they were to pay the veterinarian. She just said, "I pray that the coon didn't give him rabies."

She was so understanding that Thad almost went ahead and opened up another sore subject, that of the corn liquor business. But he didn't care to see her even more disappointed with him, at least not now. It could wait. In fact, it could be that she'd never have to know at all. Of course, that would depend on whether or not Pearly told her anything.

It would probably be best, too, if Thad didn't sell any more liquor for Dayman from now on. Dayman could find himself another salesman, or he could sell it himself. Though he felt sorry for Dayman, it wasn't as if he owed the man anything—aside from the eight dollars for the lost liquor. It wasn't as if Dayman was family, or even much of a friend.

Yet there was no denying that, in some way, he would miss his visits with Dayman, one-sided as they were. It was as if Dayman stood for a particular way of living, one that appealed to Thad—a solitary, primitive kind of existence that was close to nature and close to the bone.

For a long time—well before he ever met Dayman—Thad had pictured himself leading just such an existence and wanting nothing more. But lately something had happened to destroy that picture of his, the way that coming awake destroys a pleasant dream. Thad could not put his finger on any one thing as the cause of it. It seemed that nearly every single thing that had happened that summer had had a hand in it.

Or it could be that none of them had. It could be that it was no outside influence at all, but something inside him that had changed, something that took hold of you when you reached a certain age, and made you suddenly look at the work in a different way. Whatever it was, he didn't much like it. It made him feel like a stranger to himself. He wished he could go back somehow, retreat into the comforting world of the dream. But he knew with that cold certainty that comes upon you when the day is under way that he could not, not unless he cut himself off from the real world, the way Dayman had. And he had a feeling that Dayman had not divorced himself from the world that way deliberately, that it was something he had given up against his will, along with his arm.

18

In the morning Thad headed into the hills to hunt again. Though Momma fretted over the possibility that he might encounter another rabid animal, she couldn't deny that they needed the meat.

Thad purposely went by way of the town square in order to give Clem Cordell and the other boys a good look at the twenty-two rifle. He didn't let on that the gun was on temporary loan to him. In fact, he led the boys to believe that his daddy had sent it to him as a birthday present. When Clem pointed out that his birthday wasn't until November, Thad blithely came up with an explanation: His daddy was bound for some corner of the world so remote and uncivilized that it didn't even have a name, and that sending anything to the outside world from there would be out of the question.

Now that Thad had decided to have no more to do with selling corn liquor, Pearly Rickett's threat of watching his every move didn't concern him particularly. If the deputy wanted to waste his time traipsing through the woods on the trail of an innocent squirrel hunter, that was all right with Thad. If nothing else, it meant that Pearly would have less time to hang around his momma.

Thad also hoped that Harlan would manage to spend more time with her. If the two of them were to strike up a serious acquaintance, he wouldn't mind at all.

On the bank of the Big Sugar, Thad halted to roll up the legs of his overalls. As he straightened up, he heard someone behind him, breathlessly calling his name. He turned to see Willa approaching at a run, her hair and her dress flying out behind her.

"What are you doing here?" Thad said. "Your folks are going to—"

"I don't care!" she interrupted. "I told them I had a headache and was going home to lie down, and I don't care if'n they believed me or not. I had to warn you." She plunked herself down on an uprooted sycamore to catch her breath.

Thad sat next to her. "Warn me? About what?"

"Pearly Rickett was in the store just now, talking to Mr. Kinsley, and I overheard every word of it. Pearly said you're running whiskey for somebody named Dayman. Is that so?"

"No any more, it ain't."

"But you were? How come you never told me?"

Thad laughed. "Your folks think poorly enough of me as it is."

"I never would have let on to them, you know I wouldn't."

"Well, I guess they know now, anyway, don't they?"

"No; they were both gone. Anyway, that ain't what I come to tell you. Pearly also said that there's a federal revenue agent in town, and he's found out a couple of stills already and busted them up, and now he's fixing to do the same to your friend Dayman's. I figured you'd want to warn him."

Thad scowled. "Shoot. This revenue agent—did Pearly seem to think he knew right where to find Dayman's still?"

"Uh-huh. In fact he said the agent plans to raid it this very afternoon."

"Well, why would he tell Pearly about it?"

"I reckon he wanted Pearly's help. It sounded like the feller was afraid there might be some shooting involved."

"That'd be reason enough for Pearly to turn him down." Thad got to his feet and cradled the gun in his arm. "I got to let Dayman know. Thanks for warning me, Willa. You're a good friend."

"You ain't going to use that, are you?" she asked, glancing at the gun.

"On a squirrel or two, maybe. Not on no federal revenue agent. With any luck, we'll get Dayman's setup moved someplace else before the feller turns up. I'd best be moving now."

He started down the creek bank, but then Willa called to him again. "Thad. One other thing."

"What's that?"

"Pearly said this Dayman feller's last name is Curtiss. Ain't that what Minnie's momma said your daddy's name was?"

Thad put a hand to his forehead. His brain was having some trouble getting a firm hold on so many new developments all at once. "That's so. Pearly said his name once, but it slipped my mind. You don't—"

"Maybe, maybe not. There's lots of Curtisses in McDonald County."

Thad frowned. "How come you to know what Minnie's momma said to me anyway? You were asleep."

She smiled smugly. "Didn't I tell you I was a good actress?"

As Thad's legs splashed across the creek and scrambled up the hill on the far side, his head tried to sort out all that was going on. He'd made up his mind to have no more to do with Dayman or with the corn liquor trade, but this changed the complexion of things. He couldn't very well let the man and all his equipment fall into the hands of a federal revenue agent, who would at best destroy his means of making a living and would at worst haul Dayman himself off to jail for a year or more.

Thad wouldn't let that happen, even to somebody he scarcely knew, not if he could help it, and there was the possibility, newly realized, that Dayman might be some kind of kin. If that was so, then Dayman might well have known Thad's daddy, and be able to add something to Thad's scanty store of knowledge about the man. For all he knew, Dayman might even be John Curtiss' brother. Mrs. Brewer had made it clear that the Curtisses were not a respectable or law-abiding lot, and Dayman pretty much fit that description.

Thad didn't take a roundabout route this time. He cut straight across country at as fast a pace as he could manage. The gun was a considerable nuisance; the trigger guard kept on hanging on limbs and snagging the waist-high weeds he had to plow through from time to time.

But he didn't want to leave the gun along the way. Though he meant what he'd told Willa about not planning to shoot anyone, he figured it couldn't hurt to have something to scare a revenuer off with if he turned up sooner than expected.

Thad had promised Harlan he would never point the gun at anyone, but this was surely an exception. Besides, he might not have to actually point it. Just showing it might be enough. From what Willa had said, the federal agent didn't sound anxious to get involved in any gunplay. Obviously the man was no Randolph Scott. Thad pictured him acting more like the sheriff in that moving picture, cowardly and underhanded and unshaven. He should be easy enough to scare off.

By the time he reached Dayman's hollow, Thad's lungs were aching and he had a stabbing pain in his ribs. He didn't have Dauncey with him to announce his presence, so he just hollered as loud as he could, as he strode along the dry stream bed. "Dayman! It's me! It's Thad!" He hoped Dayman heard him. He didn't want to take the man by surprise. He didn't recall ever seeing a gun in the vicinity of the still, but Dayman surely had one concealed somewhere, and Thad didn't care to startle him into using it.

Dayman was taking a full gallon jug of corn liquor out from under the end of the copper worm and replacing it with an empty one. He scarcely glanced up as Thad approached.

Thad leaned on the twenty-two, gasping for breath. "You got to shut the still down and move it! A revenuer's fixing to raid you!"

Dayman didn't reply. He just moved over to the cooker and threw several handfuls of hickory chips into the fire.

"Didn't you hear me?" Thad shouted. "I said there's—"

"I heard you. I can't shut it down in the middle of running a batch. I worked too hard at grinding that mash to let it go to waste."

"There's going to be a lot more than corn go to waste if'n you don't get a move on. That revenuer means to bust up your still and he's liable to throw you in jail, too."

"I been in jail before. That don't scare me none."

Thad kicked at the gravel underfoot in frustration.

"You mean to tell me I practically killed myself running up here to warn you, and you ain't going to do ary a thing about it?"

"I don't reckon there's much I can do. I don't know of no other good place I can set up the still, and if'n I did, it would require a day or more to move it."

"Well, can't we just hide it till you find a place? Shoot, Dayman, we can't just sit here and wait for the revenuer to come!" Thad stood shifting about impatiently while Dayman thought it over—at least Thad assumed he was thinking it over. It could be he'd just said all he had to say on the subject. You never could tell with Dayman.

A crow rose, flapping and cawing, from a tree at the top of the ridge and Thad turned that way, wondering what had set it off. Then he heard the faint sound of dead leaves crunching and twigs snapping. "Oh, lordy," Thad breathed. He crouched next to Dayman and whispered urgently into the man's good ear, "He's here already! We'll have to scare him off! Where's your gun?"

Thad fished in his pocket for one of the twenty-two shells. Despite the panic rising in him, he took the time to pick a decent one and to slip it into the chamber carefully. It wouldn't do to have it jamming again, not now.

Before he could slide the bolt into place, though, the gun was snatched from his grasp. Alarmed, he jerked his head up. Dayman had the twenty-two by the barrel and was holding it at arm's length, the way a person will hold something rotten or distasteful. "There won't be no guns," he said harshly.

"But that agent, he's going to be armed!" Thad protested. "We can't run him off by just hollering at him!"

"It don't matter. There'll be no guns." Dayman drew his arm across his body and flung the rifle away from him. It sailed the width of the narrow hollow, rebounded off the limestone cliff, and landed with a splash in the shallow stream.

Thad was too shocked to respond, and it wasn't only the fear that Harlan's find gun was ruined that stunned him. It was also the fact that Dayman was so dead set against the use of guns. One of the few things Momma had ever told him about his daddy was that John Curtiss hated guns.

Thad tried hard to tell himself that there might be no significance in this, that probably any number of men who had fought in the Great War had an aversion to guns. But he couldn't get rid of the notion that had planted itself in his mind, any more than he could make the approaching revenue agent turn back and leave them alone.

The crunching and cracking sounds had ceased. Thad knew that the revenuer had reached the floor of the hollow and was following the stone path directly to where they stood, stupidly waiting—or at least Thad was. Dayman was methodically piling more hickory chips on the fire under the cooker, just as if disaster were not about to descend on him.

A figure in khaki britches and a white shirt with rolled-up sleeves came into sight around an outcropping of rock. Thad gasped and blinked in surprise. "Harlan!" His face broke into a relieved grin. "It's only you!"

Then his eyes and his brain took in the handgun strapped to Harlan's side, and the ax that he carried in one hand. The grin faded as the realization struck him, like the recoil of a rifle in the pit of his stomach. "Oh, lord," he breathed.

19

Harlan stopped a few yards away from the still and leaned casually on the handle of the ax. "Hello, Thad. I imagine this is a bit of a shock to you. I'm truly sorry it had to be this way. I was hoping I could locate the still on my own, without having to trick you into leading me to it." He gazed around at the high bluffs, as if admiring Dayman's choice of a location. "It's just too well hidden."

"You . . . you lied to me," Thad said. The words threatened to choke him.

Harlan cleared his throat awkwardly, apologetically. "I know it must seem that way to you. I consider it more just a bit of—what do you call it? moonshine?—that I concocted for a good reason. As I said, I'm sorry it was necessary." He turned to Dayman, who was still tossing hickory chips under the cooker, as if unaware of what was going on or, at any rate, unconcerned. "I need you to stand back now, sir," Harlan said, more in the tone of a storekeeper addressing a customer than of a lawman giving orders to a criminal.

Dayman ignored him, and went on loading chips on the fire, which was already licking up around the sides of the copper tank. Thad could hear the mash bubbling.

Steam knocked against the sides of the thump keg like someone trying to get out.

Harlan brushed past Thad, who moved unsteadily aside. "Stand back, now," he said, more loudly and more firmly, "so you don't get hurt." He prodded Dayman with the handle of the ax.

Without a word, without even looking up, Dayman backed away and stood next to his barrels full of fermenting mash. Harlan positioned himself in front of the cooker and raised the axe over his head.

"I can't let you do that, Harlan," Thad said, his voice trembling almost as much as his hands. He stooped and swept up several good-size rocks from the streambed.

Harlan lowered the ax a little and called over his shoulder, "Stay out of this, Thad. This is serious business."

"I know it is, and I'm being serious, too. If'n you don't put down that ax, I'm fixing to brain you with one of these stones. You know I can do it."

"Maybe you can," Harlan said. "But I don't think you will." He lifted the ax again.

Thad let fly with one of the rocks. Harlan's hat tumbled from his head and landed on the edge of the flaming bed of hickory chips. Harlan snatched it up and beat at the smoking brim. "Damn it all!" He whirled around to face Thad. "I asked you to stay out of this! I can overlook you selling the whiskey, but I can't overlook it if you assault an officer of the law in the performance of his duty!"

"I thought you were my friend!" Thad cried, and felt tears starting in his eyes.

"I was," Harlan replied. "I still am. Don't you see that?

What kind of friend would I be if I let you go on involving yourself in criminal activities?" He half-turned and gestured with the ax toward Dayman's still.

At that moment a frightful explosion ripped the air, like a dozen guns being fired simultaneously. Thad jumped backward instinctively, thinking, insofar as he was able to think of anything, that a bolt of lightning had descended from the cloudless sky like the wrath of God and struck the still.

Then he felt a burning sensation on his arms and his face, and he realized what had happened. The side of the copper cooker had split wide open, spewing out dozens of gallons of boiling mash. Flecks of it stuck to his skin, and he swiped at them. But the biggest part of the mash had been blocked by Harlan, who had been standing directly between him and the cooker.

Now Harlan was writhing on the ground, screaming hoarsely, the way the rabid raccoon had screamed when Thad had stoned it, only a hundred times worse. Harlan's hands clawed at his back and legs, which were coated with scalding mash. For several seconds Thad stood frozen in place, unable to think or to act. Then something in his brain kicked in and he sprang forward.

He grabbed the copper worm at the far end of the still and flung it aside, then upended the heavy wooden trough full of water, sending its contents cascading over Harlan's thrashing body, washing away most of the wet ground corn that clung to him.

Thad fell to his knees and, taking hold of the collar of Harlan's fine white shirt, ripped it off him. The skin on Harlan's back was already bright red and a mass of blisters from the hot mash. The man's dirt-smeared features were so distorted by pain that he was unrecognizable. For an instant Thad was convinced that he had been mistaken, that it hadn't been Harlan who had come up the hollow at all but the spineless, ruthless lawman of his imagination, that Harlan had not betrayed him after all. He almost laughed with relief.

But the illusion lasted no more than a second or two. Then Harlan reached out and clutched Thad's arm and murmured between clenched teeth, "Thad. Help me."

Thad pulled away in alarm. He knew that Harlan badly needed him, but how could he possibly help? He'd had no experience with helping anyone except himself. "I can't!" he protested. "I don't know what to do!" He heard Dayman come up behind him, and looked up at him helplessly. "What should I do?"

"Leave him there, for all I care," Dayman said. "I don't owe him nothing, and neither do you. All he done was use you."

"That don't matter," Thad said. "We got to do something."

"Maybe you do. I don't. I seen better men than him die." Dayman turned away.

It was hard to think with Harlan rolling around and groaning so. Thad wanted to holler at him to stop, to not demand anything of him. He clamped his hands over his ears and concentrated. Dr. Potter, who divided his time between Anderson and Pineville, would be in town today, he was pretty sure. If he could just manage to get Harlan to him somehow. But how? He tried to get Harlan to his feet , but the man wouldn't or couldn't cooperate.

Thad fetched a jar of corn liquor from Dayman's tent and poured about a third of it down Harlan's throat, hoping it would dull the pain some. It seemed to work. Harlan went on groaning softly, pitifully, but quit thrashing about so wildly.

"I'm fixing to try and get him to Dr. Potter," Thad told Dayman. "You going to help?" Dayman didn't reply. "If'n you ain't going to, then you'd best hide out someplace, and take your setup with you."

"I told you, I got no place else to go."

"What about where you spend the winter months?"

"It's no place to set up a still. If'n I can repair that boiler, I've got a good month of whiskey making to go."

"You can't make whiskey in jail," Thad reminded him, but he saw that Dayman wasn't listening. He hesitated, debating with himself, then he swallowed hard and said, "All right. I know of a place."

Without asking permission, Thad tore down Dayman's tent and fashioned a crude stretcher out of it and two stout hickory poles, with a third pole tied crossways between them at one end to keep them apart. He figured he could drag Harlan on the stretcher at least part of the way.

All he could think of to do for the burns was to keep them wet and cool. He soaked one of Dayman's quilts in the spring water, then wrapped it carefully around Harlan's torso, trying to ignore the man's cries of pain.

He laid Harlan face down on the stretcher, lifted one of the hickory poles in each hand, and set off down the streambed. The poles jumped and jerked, raising blisters on his hands, but the going wasn't too difficult until he started up the steep slope. Then, because the stretcher was tilted so sharply, Harlan kept wanting to slide off it every few yards, and Thad had to stop and pull the man's limp body back onto the canvas.

Just as he was about to despair of ever making it to the top of the ridge, Dayman came plodding up the hill. Without a word he grabbed the crosspiece in his single hand, then indicated with a curt nod of his head that Thad should take up the other end again.

Even with Dayman's help, hauling Harlan to the top of that hill was the hardest thing Thad had ever done. After each straining step upward, he was sure he would not be able to manage another, but somehow he did. His hands ached and the blisters on them stung. The sweat streamed down his arms and onto the scalded patches of skin. It was like being burned all over again. Their strength gave out a dozen times. Each time, they took a minute's rest and then forced themselves to go on.

There were things Thad needed to say to Dayman, questions he needed to ask, but he said and asked none of them, partly because he couldn't find the breath, but mostly because he couldn't find the nerve. Once he'd asked the questions that tormented him, once he'd heard the answers, he would no longer have the luxury of inventing the answers for himself.

All these years he'd been telling his momma and himself that he wanted to know who his daddy was. But now, suddenly, he wasn't so sure. If his daddy was anything like Dayman, a solitary, shiftless misfit, maybe it was better not to know. And yet, he thought, if that was so, why should it upset him? What had he ever been himself but a solitary, shiftless misfit?

They came at last to the crest of the steep hill overlooking the highway and the Little Sugar. Far below them, Harlan's green Dodge was parked on the shoulder of the road, where he had left it to follow Thad on foot. Thad halted and lowered his end of the stretcher. "I can take it from here. If'n you go into town you're liable to be arrested after what happened."

Dayman set his end down and let his arm hang limp at his side. He glanced at Harlan, who lay face down on the stretcher, twisting slowly this way and that, his moans muffled by the canvas. "I reckon he'll be all right."

Thad had the odd sensation of having played his same scene before, and then realized why. Those were practically the same words he'd said to Harlan, on their way home from the veterinarian's. Though he was no more certain of Harlan's fate than he was of Dauncey's, he said the same thing Harlan had said. "Sure. He'll be fine."

"Well," Dayman said. "I reckon you know where to find me."

Thad nodded, and shook the numbness from his arms. The movement made his raw palms hurt even more. Dayman started off, then turned back long enough to say, "You're a good boy."

Thad stared after him. As far as he could recall, no one had ever told him such a thing before, not even Momma. He wondered if it was true.

He wondered, too, as he wearily picked up the head of the stretcher again in his hurting hands and started down the hill, whether Willa would forgive him for breaking his vow and revealing the location of Sinking Spring. He wouldn't necessarily have to tell her, of course, but he suspected he would anyway. He was tired of always keeping things to himself, nearly as tired as he was of dragging the stretcher along.

It had been hard enough with Dayman carrying some of the load. Now his arms felt as though they might just come apart at the joints, like the arms of some tore-down child's doll. His feet stumbled over obstacles that weren't there. Objects swayed before his eyes as though in a high wind, but there was not even a breath of a breeze. "I can't make it, Harlan," he panted. "I can't go on."

Harlan didn't reply. But Thad knew what his answer was, all the same: "If you say you can't, you never will."

"That's easy for you to say, durn it," Thad retorted. "All you got to do is just lay there. Anyway, I don't see why I should kill myself to help you, after what you done."

And then he thought about all the other things Harlan had done, all the good things. Of course, it could be that he had done those things for the same reason Thad himself had done so many favors for touristers—to gain his trust. But Thad preferred to think not. If that was so, then maybe it was true, too, what Harlan had said about not wanting to see him involve himself in so-called criminal activities.

What had he ever done in return, for Harlan or for anyone else? For most of his life he'd thought mainly about himself. That philosophy might be all right for someone who wanted to live cut off from everybody else, the way Dayman did. But he could no longer see himself living that way.

He pried one stiff hand loose from the stretcher frame and glanced at it. The palm was rubbed raw and bleeding.

He spit on it, then on the other hand, and then took a firmer grip on the rough hickory poles. He shuffled on down the slope, repeating to himself over and over under his breath, "I can do this. I can do it. I can."

20

For a week or or two afterward, Thad's rescue of Harlan was the talk of the town, at least according to Thad's momma. Thad himself didn't go out among folks much. The reason his momma gave was that he was recuperating, and there was some truth to that. His hands, which Dr. Potter had swathed in bandages, were paining him considerably.

But the rest of the truth was that Thad was not anxious to discuss the incident—not out of modesty, but on account of there being several details he didn't care to bring up, such as the fact that he had been running corn liquor for Dayman Curtiss.

Furthermore, he wasn't sure how much Harlan would want folks to know about the matter. Though he'd quit considering Harlan his friend, he had made a promise to keep his mouth shut about the man's affairs. Technically, all the promise had involved was the fact that Harlan was an agent for a tobacco company, and that had turned out not to be a fact after all. Still, Thad felt it best if he let Harlan himself tell what he wanted told, when he was up to it.

By the time he started back to school, interest in the

rescue had faded some, but not altogether. Clem Cordell and the others were particularly eager to hear about how Thad had managed to pilot Harlan's automobile for two or three miles to the doctor's office without running into a single thing.

"There wasn't nothing to it," Thad told them. "The hard part was getting my hands unstuck from the steering wheel once I got there."

Clem laughed. "Because you were grabbing the wheel so hard, you mean?"

"No, because of the dried blood."

There was one advantage to having his hands so torn up. Clem couldn't keep on him about pitching for the Pineville Panthers in the playoffs. Clem did say that the least he could do was come to the home games and root for them.

Thad agreed to do that much. To his surprise, he found himself caught up in the contest. So, though the Panthers lost to the Lanagan Lions, it wasn't for want of enthusiastic cheering.

Eventually he heard that Harlan was up and about again, and planning to leave Pineville as soon as he could sit comfortably behind the wheel of his automobile. Thad had considered several times visiting Harlan during his convalescence, but had always put it off, not knowing whether or not Harlan would care to see him, after all that had happened. He wasn't sure whether Harlan was likely to be grateful to him for the rescue, or disgusted with him because he'd helped bring about the accident in the first place.

Thad wasn't so sure he wanted to see Harlan, either.

He wouldn't know how to act around him, what to say.

Facing Dauncey was a whole lot easier. After fifteen days went by and the dog showed no symptoms of rabies, the vet had let him come home. Though Dauncey behaved like always toward Thad, the dog wasn't quite the same as he'd been before the encounter with the raccoon. He walked with a bit of a limp, and he didn't seem inclined to go wandering off exploring in the woods the way he once did. Most of the time he hung around close to home.

To Thad's surprise, Dauncey had begun to tolerate the little beagle pup. Momma had named the pup Pearly—because, she said, it was Pearly Rickett who gave the pup to her. But Thad suspected that the beagle's big ears and pot belly also had something to do with it.

When Pearly raided Dauncey's food bowl, Dauncey let him get away with it. He also suffered the pup's attempts to play with him. Occasionally, when he thought no one was watching, he even got into the spirit of it and wrestled awhile with Pearly.

Pearly was also responsible, in a way, for Thad's repairing the porch. After the pup fell through a hole in the porch floor, Thad set about replacing the rotten boards with some old but sound ones he found in the shed. He went at it carefully, for his hands were still tender.

As he was pulling up the bad boards, he heard an automobile pull up in front of the house. Hoping it wasn't the original Pearly, he put down the hammer and turned to see. It was a green convertible. Harlan opened the door and slid carefully out, wincing a little as the motion pulled at the still-healing burns on his back and legs.

Thad noticed that the back seat of the Dodge was loaded down with suitcases and fishing gear and boxes. Harlan cleared his throat and said, "I'm heading home. I just wanted to stop and say good bye. And thanks."

"You're welcome," Thad said. "You ain't going to stay around and bust up some more stills?"

Harlan smiled wryly and shook his head. "As we say in the bureau, my cover is blown. No one is likely to tell me anything useful, now that they know I'm a revenuer."

"I didn't let on that you was."

"You didn't have to. Word gets around." Harlan sighed. "It seems to me it's a losing battle for the bureau, trying to shut down these little backwoods stills."

"Why bother, then? It ain't as if the operators are getting rich off of it."

"Because it's against the law, Thad. And because it draws in boys like you. I wish you'd promise me you won't have anything more to do with it."

"I won't be selling no more whiskey, I can promise you that. I may pay a visit to Dayman now and again, though."

"Why's that?"

"Because." Thad paused, turned a board over, and pounded at a nail. "I've got half a notion that he might be my daddy, J. D. Curtiss. I expect his full name is John Dayman Curtiss."

"Have you asked your mother about this?"

"No, sir. If'n she'd wanted me to know, she'd of told me before this. I reckon she felt he wouldn't be a good influence on me." Thad quit pounding, leaving a silence that neither of them seemed to know how to fill.

Dauncey came running around the corner of the house

with Pearly on his heels, yapping and snapping. When Dauncey saw that his foolishness was being observed, he pulled up short and the pup collided with his rear end.

"I see that Dauncey is back to his old self," Harlan said.

"Not his old self, maybe, but one just as good."

"How are your hands? The doctor said they looked pretty bad when you brought me in."

Thad flexed them. "They're fixing to be all right."

"Good enough for a farewell handshake?"

"I reckon." They shook hands, then. Thad held back a bit, not wanting to hurt Harlan, and he sensed that Harlan was doing the same. As Harlan got back behind the wheel of the Dodge, Thad said, "I meant to tell you, I'm sorry about the rifle you loaned me. Dayman throwed it in the creek. If'n it's not too tore up, I could send it to you."

Harlan waved a hand dismissively. "You keep it. Just don't use it to shoot at any revenue agents, all right?"

"Why don't you just tell them not to send around no more. We got trouble enough without them."

Harlan laughed and started up the automobile. Thad leaned forward and gingerly placed his hands on the top of the passenger door, as if to hold the vehicle in place a moment longer. "There's something I got to ask before you go."

"What's that?"

Thad looked down at the running board and scuffed at it with one foot. "All them things you done for me— letting me use the gun and the fishing rod, and lending me them clothes and all—was it all just so I'd get to trusting you, and maybe give something away?"

Harlan blew out his breath in a sort of sigh, like the question Thad had posed was a tough one. "That was part of it, I have to admit," he said reluctantly. "But it was a small part. I'll do whatever is necessary, usually, in order to enforce the law, even tell an outright lie now and then. But I'm not so good a liar, or so bad a person, that I can convince someone I'm their friend when I'm not."

Thad raised his eyes to meet Harlan's. "Randolph Scott done it, in *Outlaw Trail*. He had the bad guys thinking he was one of them."

"Well," Harlan said, "I'm no Randolph Scott. And this is no movie."

"So, we truly were friends, then?" Thad said softly.

"We truly are." Harlan put the car in gear. "I'll be seeing you, friend."

"When?" Thad called, but he doubted that Harlan heard him. He was already driving away. Thad sighed and went back to repairing the porch. By the time Momma came home from waiting tables at the café, he had all the rotten boards replaced.

"That looks real good," Momma said.

"It'll do." Thad sat down and mopped his forehead with his bandanna. "You missed Harlan James. He stopped by about half an hour ago."

"No, I didn't either miss him. He had lunch at the café. He left me a fifteen-cent tip, too, for a fifty-cent meal." Momma jingled the change in the pocket of her dress. "I must say, I'm sorry to see him go. And not just because he left big tips."

"You liked him, didn't you?"

Momma gave him a sharp sideways glance, as if trying to decide what he had in mind. "I liked his manners. And I liked how good he was to you."

"Except that he lied to me."

"Well, now, you ain't above lying your own self, as I recall."

"I know. But I was going to tell you about the corn liquor business, truly I was. And I'd already given it up, before Harlan ever came to bust up the still."

She sniffed. "Only because Pearly Ricket promised to catch you at it, I expect."

Thad blushed. "How'd you know about that?"

"Pearly told me. I guess he thought I'd be more well disposed toward him if 'n he acted like he was concerned about you."

"Were you better disposed?"

"No. I told him I wished he'd mind his own business. I also told him I didn't want to catch him spreading no gossip to that effect around town."

The dogs came charging around the corner of the house again, and this time it was Dauncey chasing the pup named Pearly, who was yelping as if his life was in imminent danger. Momma and Thad laughed at their antics.

"The vet says there'll be a threat of rabies right up to when cold weather sets in," Thad said. "You reckon Dauncey could stay in the house of a night, until then?"

"If 'n he behaves himself. He don't seem so antisocial these days. Neither do you, for that matter. I think maybe Harlan had a good influence on you."

Her words called to mind what Thad had said himself a short time before, about Dayman being a bad influence. As if Momma were reading his thoughts, she said, "When you were running whiskey for Dayman, did he every say anything to you about your daddy?"

"He never said much about much of anything. Why? Did he know my daddy?"

Momma didn't answer right away. She dug tentatively at the dirt by the porch steps with one toe, as though she were digging up the past and wasn't sure she cared to. Finally she said, "He is your daddy, Thad." She glanced up at him, as if measuring the effect her words had had on him. "You don't seem surprised."

"I ain't. I guess I'm only surprised that you took up with . . . with somebody like that."

She took a deep breath. "Well, he wasn't always like that, you know. Before he went off to the War he was bright and lively and determined to make something of himself. He wasn't sure just what. Every week it was something different, but it was always something. And then he went off to fight. He really thought of it as a way of seeing the world, I expect. Only he didn't see much of it. Mostly just troop ships and trenches and dying men. He wrote to me for a while, but then the letters stopped coming, and I thought sure he was killed in action. Then, about two years after the War ended, he turned up again, minus an arm, and minus mostly all the things I'd liked about him.

"I told myself that if'n I just took good enough care of him I might could get him back to his old self, or at least near to it. I tried, for years on end. Sometimes he seemed fixing to get better, to climb out of whatever dark hollow his mind had fallen into, but always he'd slip back again, like he just couldn't make it with only one arm, even with me helping. Finally I had to admit that nothing I could do would make any difference. So I let him go." She wiped at her eyes, and took another deep breath.

"Why didn't you ever tell me any of that before?"

"I was afraid you might hunt him up, if'n I did, and I didn't want that. I didn't want you expecting something more from him than he could give, the way I done. And I didn't want you turning out like him. When I seen you spending more and more time off by yourself, doing lord knew what, it worried me. I was afraid you might be taking after him, that you might never amount to nothing."

Thad nodded. "Well, seeing that still blow up that way got rid of any notion I ever had about going into the corn liquor business. I believe I'll take up something less dangerous, like robbing banks." He laughed at Momma's startled look. "That's just a joke me and Harlan shared."

"I'm glad to hear that. Since you know his sense of humor, maybe you can tell me whether or not he was joking with me earlier on."

"Wh;, what did he say?"

"He said 'When I come back here, it'll be as a tourist, not a lawman,' or words to that effect."

"He said that?"

Momma nodded. "You reckon he really means to come back?"

"I guess so," Thad said, "but I can't say for sure. That's the trouble with a lie. Once a body has told you one, you can't be certain whether or not to believe anything after that."

21

The following day at school, Mrs. Mitchell announced that tryouts for the play would be held that afternoon. Willa proved once and for all just how good an actress she was. All day long in class she seemed cheerful and unconcerned. Thad overheard her blithely telling Betsey Morgan how she just didn't have time to be in the play, she was so occupied with helping out at the hardware store, and furthermore getting paid for it. She was very convincing.

On every other day Willa had waited around after the last class to say goodbye to Thad. Today she was nowhere to be seen. In the hall Thad came across Minnie Brewer, who was fetching a cup of water from the drinking fountain.

"Oh, I know where she is all right," Minnie said. "She's in the girls' room, crying her eyes out."

"About the play?" Thad said.

Minnie nodded grimly. "You know, she could've been in it if'n it wasn't for you."

"Me? I didn't do nothing."

Minnie slugged him on the arm, hard. "Anything."

"All right, I didn't do anything."

"That's right," said Minnie. "You didn't." She turned on her heel and headed for the girls' room before Thad could ask her what she meant by that.

But as he walked slowly across the schoolyard, the answer came to him. What he hadn't done was to speak up on Willa's behalf, to protest to Willa's folks. He'd offered to, but only halfheartedly, knowing that Willa would tell him not to bother. A good friend would have gone ahead and done what he could to make a difference.

Well, it was never too late to try. He changed course and headed for Houseman's Hardware. The dog days of late summer had passed now, and the heat had let up some, but still they'd had not a trace of rain. Every now and again the sky got low and dark, promising a storm, but it never delivered. This was one of those deceptive days. There was even an occasional flash of lightning off to the south, but that didn't mean anything.

Willa's momma was behind the counter, waiting on Fate Norwood, who was buying equipment for an indoor toilet. When Thad came through the door, Mrs. Houseman gave him a look so disapproving that he nearly turned back. Instead he forced a smile and murmured softly to himself, "I can do this."

As soon as Fate was out of the store, Mrs. Houseman turned to Thad. "What do you want?"

"Justice, ma'am," Thad said. The words sounded curiously familiar, but it took him a moment to realize why. They'd been spoken by Randolph Scott in *Outlaw Trail*.

Mrs. Houseman blinked, obviously taken aback. "I beg your pardon?"

Thad plunged forward. "You done Willa an injustice, ma'am. You accused her of disobeying by going to the moving pictures with me, and you punished her for it."

"She did go to the pictures with you," Mrs. Houseman said. "Didn't she?"

"No, ma'am. We did meet up in Anderson, but it was

purely by accident. You see, I went there with my friend Harlan James—"

"The revenue agent?"

"Yes, ma'am. Naturally when I seen Willa come out of the moving pictures, I thought it would be rude not to say hello. I reckon somebody seen us, and just assumed we was there together all along."

"Oh." Mrs. Houseman fiddled with the spool of wrapping twine, seemingly at a loss for a reply. Finally she said, "Well . . . why were you and Mr. James in Anderson, then?"

"We was fishing on Indian Creek."

"After dark?" she said incredulously.

"Yes, ma'am. We was goosing the fish."

"I beg your pardon?"

"Ain't you heard about goosing? You set a light in the boat and stir up the water, and the fish jump right in the boat."

"Really? They just jump in?"

"Yes, ma'am. So, as you can see, it wasn't none of Willa's doing at all, and she shouldn't be made to suffer for it. I hope you'll see your way clear to let her try out for that play."

Mrs. Houseman fiddled thoughtfully with the twine. "Well. I'll talk to my husband about it, that's all I can promise you." She looked up and, quite unexpectedly, Thad saw a glint of amusement in her eyes. "Usually if I am persistent I can make him see things my way."

Thad suppressed a grin. "I expect you can." He reached out and gave her hand a quick, businesslike shake. "Thank you, ma'am, for being so fair and reasonable."

She gave a tentative, fleeting smile. "You're quite welcome." As Thad was going out the door, she added, "By the way, Mr. James told us all about how you saved his life."

Thad winced. He hadn't wanted them to know about the corn liquor business. "He did?"

"Yes. It was a courageous thing."

Thad shrugged. "Anybody would have done the same."

"I'm not sure everyone could have. That surely must have been a poor excuse for a camp stove he had."

"Ma'am?" Thad said, puzzled.

"Well, it ought not to have blown up and burned him the way it did. Perhaps he didn't know how to use it properly, a city fellow like him."

Thad bit his lip and nodded. "I reckon that was it," he said, and ducked out the door before he lost the ability to control his laughter. As he started up the sidewalk, he noticed for the first time that Mr. Houseman had torn down the dilapidated storage shed that had stood—or rather leaned—in the space between the hardware store and the drugstore. Where the shed had been was a long, narrow rectangle of barren, dried-up dirt.

On a whim, Thad stepped off the sidewalk and onto the dirt. Folks said that if you stood on a patch of strange ground for the first time and made a wish, that wish was certain to come true. He had told Willa that he wasn't much of a one for making wishes, and that was so. But that was before he had met Harlan and come to find out about all the things there were in the world that a person might wish for.

Thad closed his eyes and tried to think of what one

thing he wanted most of all. The concept was new to him, though, and he found he couldn't make up his mind. So far as he knew, there was no law that said you had to wish for something for yourself, either, and when he got to considering all the things he'd like for his momma to have, or Willa, that made it even harder.

In the end, he decided that there was also no law saying that you had to make the wish right away. Maybe it was best if he thought it over for a while before settling on something.

As he stepped back onto the sidewalk, something wet struck his arm. He startled and brushed the wetness away, imagining for an instant that he was being splattered again with hot mash. Then he realized what it was. Rain.

It came down faster and harder, now, forming clear, gemlike beads on the dusty sidewalk and sending up a peculiar bitter odor from the pavement on the square. Thad didn't bother to run for cover. Instead he walked slowly home though the downpour, relishing the feel of something besides salty sweat trickling down his back.

He relished, too, the story Harlan had told Mrs. Houseman to explain how the accident had come about. Though Harlan had not been in McDonald County for long, apparently it had been long enough for him to get the hand of that valued Ozark skill, embroidering the truth. It was a skill that certainly could come in handy at times. But, like the making of corn liquor, it could prove dangerous.

A bit of moonshine might seem harmless enough, but if you weren't careful it was liable to build up and expand into something that blew up in your face. Maybe it was time he gave up moonshining, just as he had given up running whiskey. It would not be an easy thing to do, but he had done a lot of difficult things lately, just by telling himself that he could.

Besides, wasn't he already headed in the right direction? Up to now, when he had stretched the truth a bit it was always in an attempt to talk his way out of trouble, or to make himself look better in the eyes of others, or as a way of being entertaining. Just now, though, when he'd told Mrs. Houseman that slightly altered version of the truth, it had been for a different purpose—the same purpose Harlan had in mind, no doubt, when he told the tale about the mythical camp stove. It was in order to make life a little easier for somebody else.

There was no doubt about it, he was already making progress. He could do this. He could definitely do this.

BLA   72258

Blackwood, Gary L.
Moonshine

TECUMSEH MIDDLE SCHOOL
LIBRARY MEDIA CENTER

DEMCO